St. Louis Community College

Library

5801 Wilson Avenue
St. Louis, Missouri 63110

Dmitri Shostakovich

DMITRI SHOSTAKOVICH

IVAN MARTYNOV

Dmitri
Shostakovich

THE MAN AND HIS WORK

Translated from the Russian
by T. Guralsky

GREENWOOD PRESS, PUBLISHERS
NEW YORK

PREFACE

THIS BOOK WAS WRITTEN in the winter of 1942. Recalling my efforts at the time, I must express gratitude to those whose advice and instruction proved invaluable in bringing it to completion. First and foremost among them there was Dmitri Dmitrievich Shostakovich who had so much of interest to tell me and who so kindly agreed to review the manuscript. Then there was the music critic Grigory Mikhailovich Shneerson whose comradely aid was more than welcome during the final editing. Lastly, there was my teacher, Professor Arnold Alexandrovich Alshvang, whose powers of perception have exercised strong influence upon myself and other musicologists, and who helped me to solve many a problem which arose as I wrote this book.

To write about Shostakovich is at once easy and exacting. Easy—because his merits are undeniable; exacting—because the key to his treasure house is often so difficult to grasp. Years of study of his music and my sincere admiration for it made me confident that a book like this could be written. I cannot, of course, claim that it has exhausted the subject. If I have succeeded in creating a portrait of the composer in broad but recognizable outlines, I shall consider my task fulfilled.

IVAN MARTYNOV.

Moscow, U.S.S.R.

CONTENTS

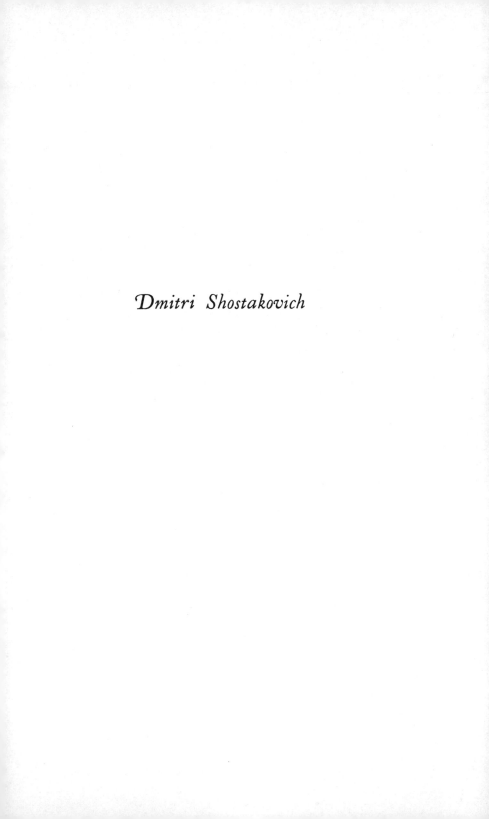

Dmitri Shostakovich

CHAPTER I

THE ROAD BEGINS

Dmitri Dmitrievich Shostakovich was born on September 25, 1906 into the family of an engineer in St. Petersburg. As a child he displayed no special musical talent and no one could have guessed that he was destined to become a famous composer. His parents, however, were ardent lovers of music, which they regarded as essential in the upbringing of their children. Dmitri received his first piano lesson at the age of nine.

His mother was his first teacher. Just as patiently and lovingly some years previously she had taught the future composer's two elder sisters to play the piano. The boy made rapid progress and soon began to study at the Glasser School of Music. Not content to play the compositions of others only, he tried his hand at music making. Noteworthy is the fact that even in those youthful first attempts he sought to respond musically to the events of the times. The spirit of 1914 emanated from his poem "Soldier." The revolution was mirrored in his "Revolutionary Symphony" and "Funeral March in Memoriam to the Fallen Heroes of the Revolution." Needless to say these were the timid probings of a beginner, but the boy persevered with such an earnestness and an eagerness for creation that finally his talents could no longer escape the attention of his family. They went into council and decided that he should become a professional musician.

This was in the Autumn of 1919. Times were hard in Russia and particularly so in Petrograd, where Shostakovich continued to reside. Winter was approaching. Fuel and food were scarce. . . . But in the great cold houses there dwelt a staunch and valiant people. Undismayed, they labored for the welfare of their country. Life went on within the walls of the Petrograd Conservatory where famous teachers of music continued to impart their experience and knowledge to young musicians. Adolescent Shostakovich too came here to study.

Dmitri played before the venerable director of the conservatory, Alexander Konstantinovich Glazounov, famous Russian composer and favorite pupil and friend of Rimsky-Korsakov. He was prompt to recognize the gifts of the youngster and on his advice Shostakovich from the outset applied himself to two subjects: pianoforte and the theory of composition. Glazounov watched over the development of the young composer, encouraged and supported him, secured him a monthly stipend which he continued to receive throughout his studies at the conservatory. It was thus that a representative of Russia's old school of music, a descendant of the "Mighty Handful" (Balakirev, César Cui, Rimsky-Korsakov, Borodin and Mussorgsky) welcomed and encouraged the first steps of this remarkable musician of our time.

Shostakovich made light of difficulties where others toiled uphill for years. But he had a tremendous zest for hard work which bore fruit in his growing mastery of piano technique. Professor Leonid Nikolayev, his teacher, was quick to appreciate his artistic individuality. In the short space of four years Shostakovich went through the full course of the conservatory and in 1923 brilliantly completed his training as a pianist. At the graduation concert he rendered one of Beethoven's most difficult sonatas, the formidable Opus 106.

Shostakovich's laurels as a pianist were plentiful and instantly attained. He attributed more importance, however, to composition which he had studied under Maximilian Steinberg, an outstanding representative of the Rimsky-Korsakov school. The principles of the latter undoubtedly strongly influenced the young composer in his formative period. It is true that he subsequently departed far from the traditions of this school, but one must not forget that many a daring innovator was bred on Rimsky-Korsakov theorics. If we recall that Igor Stravinsky and Serge Prokofieff came from the Petersburg school, there is nothing really incongruous in the evolution of a Shostakovich from the traditions of Korsakov and Glazounov. From Maximilian Steinberg he derived high professional skill (in the spirit of Rimsky-Korsakov who despised dilettantism in any guise) and the best that one of Russia's finest schools of music could give.

A good deal of the student composer's time was taken up by his assignments in harmony, counterpoint, fugue construction and instrumentation. The practice of so-called free composition was begun only in the final years of the conservatory course. Shostakovich was not privileged to disregard the rules. Conscientiously he labored over every task and invariably earned the praise of his exacting tutor. This alone failed to satisfy him. His creative urge required an outlet. Between classes he more and more often devoted himself to various compositions.

During his period of study at the conservatory, he wrote: 8 preludes for the pianoforte, a theme and variations for orchestra, 2 pieces based on the fables of Krylov, 3 fantastic dances, a suite for two pianofortes, an F-minor orchestra scherzo, a trio for pianoforte, violin and violoncello, 3 pieces for violoncello and, finally, his First Symphony. Ever critical of his work, he subsequently published only the "Fantastic Dances" and the symphony, regarding all else as mere trial. We shall not quarrel with the author's severity. Suffice it to say that even externally these early compositions bore many features characteristic of his later works: predilection for instrumental music and sense of humor (two scherzos for orchestra and the "Krylov Fables").

An idea of Shostakovich's early work may be gained from his "Fantastic Dances," small pieces for the pianoforte which have lost none of their charm to the present day. Characteristic of him here are the lightness of touch and graceful humour as well as the imagery: the drollery of the first dance, the lyrical capriciousness of the second and particularly the grotesque "zig-zags" of the third. The "galloping" miniature rhythms, the unexpected harmonic changes and turns of melody anticipated many a later page of Shostakovich.

In the life of every great artist there comes a period of crisis. The pupil of yesterday reaches the threshold of independence. Eagerly he regards his surroundings in a new light, searches for *his own* theme, *his own* world of artistic images. At last he evolves a work which captures the attention of its listeners; they sense here something that is new, somethir.g that is original. Though later and more mature works may dim these creations, the latter nonetheless preserve their inspiring freshness and youthful charm for all time.

Such a composition was Shostakovich's First Symphony. Completed in his senior year at the conservatory, it may be said to sum up the period of his studies. Shostakovich's development as a composer is remarkable for its intensity. At the age of 13 he wrote his first large work—an F-minor Scherzo for orchestra. Six years later he brought forth the score of his First Symphony which earned him world fame. What a vast distance he had traveled in the few years of his studies! How earnest must have been the efforts and strenuous the application of this modest student of Maximilian Steinberg! His studies, moreover, proceeded under harrowing conditions. His father died leaving the entire family on his hands. He was compelled to interrupt his creative work to play in the cinemas for a living. But his talent and youth gained the upper hand. His First Symphony was given its initial performance in the Great Hall of the Leningrad Philharmonic on May 12, 1926 under the baton of Nikolai Malko. Soon afterwards it was broadcast from Moscow. In the following year it was performed for the first time abroad. Since then it has been presented to music lovers again and again under the baton of such world-famous conductors as Toscanini, Koussevitzky, Stokowski, Bruno Walter and others.

Fame came to Shostakovich on the day after the premiere of his First Symphony. His debut was indeed a remarkable one. Unlike most budding composers, he had come out with a grand symphonic score. Brilliantly orchestrated, it captivated the audience by its temperament and bold flight of artistic fancy. It was not the dogma of the academy, but his inner urge for expression, his penetrating

5

intuition and desire for rational means of attaining the essence of polyphony which prompted those forms chosen by Shostakovich at the first milestone of his career. It was this which rendered the work enduring. The First Symphony has stood the test of time. How many symphonic scores have faded into oblivion in the years that have passed since the appearance of Shostakovich's First!

The importance of this work, on the other hand, has grown immeasurably. Fingering the pages of the score again and again we find our interest rekindled every time by the familiar passages, and we discover ever fresh and remarkable things about them, currents and undercurrents that escaped first notice. Shostakovich's First Symphony has become a classic work of the modern symphonic repertory.

The very first strains compel the listener's attention. An imperious flourish from muted trumpet, the sombre, strangely dove-like utterance of a bassoon—an extraordinary, even bizarre, opening for a symphony! But then the movement is interrupted by wary chords of the woodwinds. The flourish is sounded again (the theme now carried by the clarinet). It is seconded by the bassoon theme which has now lost its rhythmic distinctiveness and is carried by a solo violoncello. Contrasting elements of sound are intensified and engender growing uncertainty. The melodic images seem to disintegrate and the impression is created that the composer is vainly seeking to emerge from an enchanted circle, to grasp upon a single and major idea beyond its confines. Sharp fragments of melody are handed from instrument to instrument. Short chromatic passages give way to images energetic and yet vague.

All is graphically emphasized in this remarkable introduction. There is the irony of various turns of melody. More emphatic is the spasmodic, automatic movement of marionette images which recall certain pages of Tchaikovsky—the score of his Nutcracker Suite and particularly the nocturnal sortie against the forces of the Mouse King. This spasmodic mood emerges gradually, almost covertly, in Shostakovich's First Symphony. In a number of his later works it is more boldly and definitely introduced and assumes fresh aspects mechanically grotesque.

The introductory Allegretto is the seed from which sprouts the music of the entire symphony. Here one can sense the guiding force of creative thought which drives determinedly towards its goal. The pattern of the symphony's development strives to envelop and overcome the sombre and troubled hues of the introductory melodic images.

The main theme of the first movement sounds an answer to the troubled and questioning introduction. There is a crisp march, a seedling of an earlier melodic grain in the first measures. Slender though it is, this little reed is lively and bright in colour. Swift and light, it is marked by delicate instrumentation and subtle shading.

The march is suddenly interrupted by the familiar flourish of the trumpet. Its challenge calls forth a second theme, a measured, though lilting waltz luxuriant in counterpoint. Here again impulsiveness merges with fragility, again the orchestral colors are clear and fresh.

In the laconic exposition of the First Symphony there is no sharp dramatic conflict of two themes. One may rather say that its two themes are related, differing in genre but similar in mood. The middle section is built up on a contrapuntal union of both subjects of the exposition (the

7

second subject is severely deformed in the process, loses its fluency, grows angular and distended).

It is in the elaboration of his musical ideas that the polyphonic skill of Shostakovich is best shown. This, however, does not necessarily imply mere adeptness in combining melodies, as some critics are inclined to believe.

The alternation of the themes occurs at very short intervals and their roles are frequently reversed. In the final episode the motion wanders and we gradually return to where we began—a state of uncertainty. Once again there is the fanfare, the whisper of a flute, the mutter of violoncellos and a dry brusque pizzicato. . . . The musical action runs to a standstill, the circle closes.

The dramatic development of the first movement of the symphony is a striving to overcome the initial mood of sombre uncertainty, a struggle with inertia to release the forces of action and movement. But all was in vain. It was not impulse and will that triumphed, but the spasmodic movement of marionettes. A world of masquerades shutting out the wider vistas from human thought. . . . The idea was daringly conceived and required great effort of will for its consummation. To achieve his end, the composer counterposed the contrasting movements of his symphony which were to evolve something that was new, something that would carry the listener away from the emotional enclave of the opening movement.

Such was the Scherzo of the second movement—continuously in motion, its rhythm impetuous and swift. The main theme of the Scherzo, one of Shostakovich's finest melodic inventions, is bold, sharp, full of humor, temperamental and unconstrained in its development.

The second theme of the Scherzo is a tranquil melody

8

close to the element of song (in this case lyrical). The composer displays true virtuosity in the development of his themes. Juggling with his first theme from one instrument to the other, from the low register of the bassoons to the high-ringing register of the pianoforte, he brings to mind the scene of cheerful crowds, glimpses of multitudes of laughing faces. Entirely different associations are evoked by the second theme (carried by two flutes accompanied by the rustling tremolo of violins). We visualize the spacious valley of a river in the steppes with suggestions of the infinite variety of life. The breath-taking pace of the round dance, the lyrical calm of contemplation are both echoed here. Particularly significant is the union of the two themes in the final passage of the Scherzo. This is the culminating point in the development, a synthesis of life in two different aspects.

In this palpitating Scherzo, however, the composer again failed to overcome completely the temptation of the marionettes. There is something reminiscent of the introduction in the peculiar canon of violoncellos and double-basses which begins the Scherzo. The same intonations slip through lizard-like into the melodic current of the second theme. At the terminating velocities of the themes there is a sudden interruption in the shape of three pianoforte chords and the ensuing silence is palpably charged with spasmodic and perplexing uncertainty. These features, however, disclose a direct relation between the separate movements of the symphony; though varied and contrary in nature they are stages in the development of a single idea.

The Scherzo is brilliantly orchestrated. The composer's wit for novel orchestral combinations is inexhaustible. A

9

unique color is contributed by the frequent use of the pianoforte. The very first entrance of this instrument sounding the main theme in bright unison brings something fresh and unusual to the score. Equally unexpected and original are the rolling chromatic scales (at the beginning of the reprise). Superb are the three A-minor chords relieving the full-blown *tutti* of the orchestra. Its remarkable orchestration, vividness and temperament render the Scherzo almost the best part of the symphony.

The third part—Lento—begins with a lyrical flow of melody. Vast and calm, its main theme, carried by an oboe, is set off against the even rustling of violins. The character of this melody links it with the main theme of the first part. It is reiterated in the orchestra's *tutti*, though here graced with expressive counterpoint.

The motifs of the three preceding movements attain fresh significance in the brilliant Finale of the symphony. Here the initial mood of the first movement is at length overcome. Dynamic and swift, the Scherzo is enriched by the lyricism of the Lento. The Finale harbors that energy and decisiveness which can barely be recognized in the fragmentary introduction. Here all doubts are dispelled, all contradictions resolved. Such is the final and determinant conclusion of the symphony.

The Finale is preceded by a small pathetic passage linking it with the slow movement. A clarinet suddenly sounds the main theme which in character somewhat resembles that of the introduction. It is more dynamic, however, continuous and flavored with the character of the Scherzo. The beginning of the Finale is pervaded by the rapid flow of this theme, handed from instrument to instrument in constantly varying timbre.

The second theme is a broad and sonorous melody appearing at once in the mighty *tutti* of the orchestra. It attains even more grandeur in the final episodes of the symphony. The movement gains momentum, grows in volume and finally dissolves in a flood of stirring sounds bringing the entire work to a solemn and festive conclusion.

Shostakovich's First Symphony is closely linked with world, and particularly with Russian, symphonic music. There is much in it that has evolved from the traditions of the Rimsky-Korsakov school. Here too it is not difficult to discern the traces of Prokofieff and some Scriabin influences. All these, however, have been colored in the prism of a strong individuality. This explains the unusual emotional content and style. The symphony owes its originality also to the melody pattern and unique orchestration. Its natural sagacity, its swift rhythms, impetuousness and sharp humor easily identify the author.

Shostakovich's gift for symphonic thought, indicated by the unity and masterful development of his musical ideas, were shown in his First Symphony. The melodic roots were planted in the very first measures of the introductory Allegretto, from which sprouted the first (and consequently—the second) theme of the Allegro, the Lento theme and the main theme of the Finale. This affinity is less easily discerned in the Scherzo, but here too one can perceive certain tonal relations. In a great variety of passages he has thus achieved continuity and monolithic unity, a primary condition of musical logic.

This musical logic influences the conception of the entire symphony. We have already discussed the content of the first movement. Its principal features, however, grow more evident in the succeeding movements. The marching stride of the main theme is relieved by the vigorous Scherzo. The lyric second theme predominates in the expansive melody of the Lento. It is only in these two movements that the vital motifs come into their own. They had been evident before, but veiled by the spasmodic marionette images. Guided by logic, the composer launches his Finale from here.

There is nothing that is particularly profound in this symphony, and that is fortunate. A young man of seventeen is rarely profound. Few at that age command the experience of the philosopher, and what can be worse than the affectation of some young composer who would don the toga of the philosopher!

The symphony owes its character to the construction of the melodies, to the polyphonic web of ideas and the brilliance of the orchestration. Characteristic too is the composer's rejection of all that is redundant, of all that might dim the expression of his principal ideas. The polish of the mature Shostakovich, of course, is still lacking, but the prerequisites for his further development are clearly to be discerned in the fine orchestration, the subtle fabric of his polyphonic patterns, their clear-cut condensation.

The latter is particularly important. Shostakovich is a gifted composer, one who is guided by an iron chain of logic. At a certain phase in the development of his constructive principles Shostakovich proved himself akin to the western European *linearists*.[1] He accepted their principles with reservations, however. The symphony of the young composer is well-knit and austerely balanced, but far from

---

[1] A linearist is a composer who evolves several subjects simultaneously and presents them in an unbroken parallel flow, at times with little regard to their interrelation—*Trans.*

the studied combination of conventional elements for the sake of effect alone.

Its imagery too is original. The grotesque is introduced at the beginning. More vital is his Scherzo, which subsequently prompted many of his best pages. His lyricism unfolds from the meditative to poignant pathos. The grotesque and the lyric, irony and perturbation—all these are felt in the later works of the composer as well.

Aside from the positive qualities of the First Symphony there were certain things here which eventually led the composer astray. The construction of initial passages in later works acquired purely abstract and conventional significance. Somewhat overdone, the grotesque attained the proportions of mockery and his means of expression grew highly exaggerated. The very flight of his fantasy tended to lead him to thoughtlessness, to the superficial, and this was indeed the case in certain of his compositions. Years later, however, his flight of fancy attained truly Mozartian clarity in his Sixth Symphony.

His First Symphony may be said to have brought Shostakovich to a cross-roads. From here he could have departed in two directions. It is certain, however, that the symphony was of particular importance in his artistic development, concluding as it did his period of study and launching him upon the road of further development.

The Soviet symphony in those years had not yet come into its own. Of new symphonic works there were few and mostly written by composers of the older generation, masters who had launched their careers before the revolution. First and foremost among them was Nikolai Myaskovsky who finished his remarkable Sixth Symphony in 1923. This composer for the first time in the history of symphonic music strove honestly and vividly to develop the motif of the revolution, to define his attitude to the great events of history and his position in the new world. Other remarkable works of the times were V. Shcherbachev's Second Symphony, echoing in music the lyrical poetry of Alexander Blok (whose moods found reflection also in the symphonic prologue to the drama "Unknown Lady," written by the young composer V. Kryukov) and "Symphonic Monument" by Mikhail Gnessin, who had conceived his composition as a story of the revolutionaries of 1905, as a monument to their heroism. Varied though these works may be (Myaskovsky's problem of remodeling the human consciousness, the Blok "fearsome world" influence discernible in the work of Shcherbachev, the striving to surmount individualism and to conceive of greater historical and social values as evidenced in the work of Gnessin), there is a close affinity between them. All of them evolved from the pre-revolutionary trends of modern Russian art, trends which they overcame either in the subjective-psychological manner of Shcherbachev or by probing for a fresh and revolutionary basis, in the manner of Myaskovsky and Gnessin. One and all, they reflect the regeneration of the older composers' consciousness.[2]

Shostakovich had no such experience. His symphony,

---

[2] N. Myaskovsky describes the process of this regeneration in his autobiographical notes published in the journal "Soviet Music" in 1936. "It was my hazy world outlook at the time which led me to the conception of the Sixth Symphony, so strange to me now with its motif of 'sacrifice,' of 'expiation' and its peculiar apotheosis at the end of 'blissful existence.' But the agitation which I experienced in the creation of this symphony and the ardor with which it was written renders it dear to me. Now, too, for that matter, it seems capable of capturing the attention of its listeners, judging by its renditions here and its ever more frequent renditions abroad, particularly in America."

perhaps, was the first exposition of artistic principles of the younger generation of composers. In his case (as in that of other composers of his age) modernism had not formed a stage of his development and could not, so to speak, be jotted down as an item in his biography. In his work its manifestations were prompted by the artistic significance of its style in the recent past. The dynamic origin of a new life is the predominant motif in the First Symphony. Its strange, perhaps awesome shadings did not elude the young composer's perception. This was typical of Shostakovich's symphonic composition at that phase in the development of Soviet music.

CHAPTER II

BREEZE FROM THE WEST

Soon after he had completed the score of the First Symphony, Shostakovich entered upon a period of crisis. According to his admissions he was dissatisfied with his new work and probed doggedly for new paths. It seemed to him that he was held in check by scholastic traditions.

Abandoning composition for a time, he devoted himself energetically to the piano, gave many recitals and in 1927 participated in the Chopin pianoforte contest in Warsaw. Before his departure for Poland, he and other Soviet pianists who were to play in Warsaw, gave a recital in the Large Hall of the Moscow Conservatory. Professor Arnold Alshvang who was present later wrote that all who had heard Shostakovich that evening would undoubtedly remember his fine rendition of the great Polish master, earnest and genuine throughout and innocent of "salon" affectations. . . . Another critic observed that the young pianist had "raised the poetic essence of Chopin to first place . . ." Shostakovich did very well at the contest, met all the requirements and only in the final concerts yielded first place to his compatriot Lev Oborin, who was adjudged the winner.

Soon after he graduated from the conservatory, Shostakovich felt that his knowledge of musical literature was insufficient. According to his admission, he was thoroughly familiar only with the field of pianoforte music. His knowledge of chamber music and symphonic scores was vague. He recalled that during a sight-reading examination on one occasion he and one of his comrades had been called upon to play the E-minor Symphony of Brahms in four hands. They found it difficult and had to stop frequently. Finally, they were compelled to admit that they had never heard this symphony before. Glazounov, who was present, smiled goodnaturedly and observed "How lucky you are! There are so many wonderful things you have yet to hear."

Consumed with curiosity, Shostakovich became engrossed in the music that was new to him. Everything attracted his attention: the works of the Russian and Western classical composers, modern music and that of other epochs. His outlook broadened and his creative potentiality increased. After some eighteen months of hard work he returned to composition and began to write with feverish haste as though striving to compensate for time lost. His compositions appeared one after the other. In the space of three or four years he wrote an opera, two symphonies, two ballet scores, a pianoforte sonata, an octet and many smaller pieces.

The composer's youthful ardor and enviable creative capacity prompted the most daring experiments. His harmonic acumen, bold melodic lines and inclination to sequential construction attained hypertrophical forms. Urban grotesquery and even mockery came ever more clearly to the fore. It seemed that the young and spirited artist had donned a mask of scepticism, had deliberately departed from the human element for a world of warped and angular

17

imagery. Every note from his pen, however, bore the stamp of great talent. Despite numerous influences he had preserved a hand of his own. He was invariably identified by his music.

The motives for this unexpected and perhaps odd evolution of Shostakovich's creative power will be better understood by reviewing the musical life of Leningrad in the latter twenties.

Music lovers of Leningrad in 1924–1929 were particularly drawn to the innovations of Western music. The war and the blockade had isolated Soviet musicians from Western European music for a long time. In 1924 a series of modern "Western Music Evenings" were arranged to acquaint concert goers with the works of contemporary Western composers. "Modern Music Associations" were soon formed in Moscow and Leningrad for the same purpose, but on a large scale. These associations not only united most of the well-known composers, but also exercised an influence upon the young composers. Particularly intensive were the activities of the Leningrad association, which here strongly influenced the choice of repertory of the opera houses and concert organizations. The Leningrad Philharmonic more and more often rendered the works of Stravinsky, Hindemith, Krenek, Schoenberg, Milhaud and others. The opera houses consecutively produced "Distant Chimes" by Franz Schrekker, "Leap Through the Shadow" and "Johnny" by Ernst Krenek, "Wozzeck" by Alban Berg and others. Warmly received in Leningrad were the guest performances of Paul Hindemith, who arrived with his quartet, of Darius Milhaud and Jean Wiener.

The innovations of western music penetrated to the music schools and were studied ever more carefully. A considerable part of the students found their musical *credo* here. Thirsting for new things, they experimented with new sound combinations and, unnoticed by themselves, strayed ever further from the wholesome basis of the Russian school. This was determinedly opposed by A. Glazounov and M. Steinberg who stoutly championed the classic ideals.

During his years at the conservatory Shostakovich was scarcely touched by the "modern" influences. All the stronger did they affect him after graduating from the conservatory. Striving to free himself from the scholastic traditions he looked to the new masters for support. Facility in composition enabled him quickly to assimilate various styles. His circle of interests was great enough. The polyphonic skill and sceptical grotesquery of Stravinsky, the linear principles of Hindemith and many other things were reflected in the new work of the young composer. So seriously was he drawn to western music that in 1930 he wrote two compositions to be included in Dressel's opera "Columbus," then produced by the Leningrad Opera House. Excellently orchestrated, the "Entr'acte" and "Finale," Opus 22, were so warmly received by the audience that they eclipsed the music of Dressel's opera.

The fact that the new compositions of Shostakovich delighted the modern music circles unquestionably accelerated his evolution towards the excesses of formalism. Highly gifted, he as yet lacked well defined artistic principles and so, as his teacher M. Steinberg put it, "he fell under the influence of people who preached and advocated the principles of the extreme West." This determined the character of his work for a number of years.

His first experiment in the new style was the pianoforte

19

Sonata Opus 12. Today the composer himself regards it as one of the least successful of his works. Its music bears the traces of various influences. Quite ecclectic, it combines elements of Prokofieff, Stravinsky and even of Scriabin. Poor melodically, its harmonic pattern abounds in harsh dissonances essentially atonal. Perceptible here and there is the impulsive beat of Shostakovich's initial principle. Automatic movement predominates, however, and somewhat reminds one of the famous "Toccata" of Serge Prokofieff.

The sonata was at once followed by "Aphorisms," a series of small pieces for the piano, and a string octet. Among the "Aphorisms" there are pages of subtle and graceful lyrics ("Elegy" and "Cradle Song"), but most of them are dry and abstract. This is even more true of the string octet (particularly of the second movement—the Scherzo). The composer here gives vent to pretentious grotesquery. The dynamic development which struck the listener in his First Symphony is lacking in the "mechanical" music of the Scherzo. Shostakovich displayed great ingenuity in the conception and technique of his polyphonic patterns, but all this is "music meant for the eye."

Shostakovich reached the peak of his formalistic tendency in the opera "The Nose," composed between the summers of 1927 and 1928. The salient features of this opera are its scenic eccentricity, the composer's desertion of customary operatic genres and the studied alogism of its musical content. It was precisely here that his formalistic innovations, and deformation of genre and musical logic attained their culminating point.

The composer himself had believed that the music of this opera was not to be sufficient unto itself, was not to play an independent role, but was to depend on the libretto to carry it over. Those who have heard the opera would find it difficult to agree with him. The opera's essence lay precisely in the independence of its musical structure. The score impresses one as a unique anthology of musical experiments, at times linked with the action on the stage, but in the main stunning the listener with its paradoxicality and novelty. The composer could not have been seriously thinking of "putting his text over" at all. That is perfectly obvious, because the text was mostly so meaningless that "putting it over" was neither necessary nor desirable. Very often the manner of execution itself obscured the text. This was true, for example, of the celebrated octet of old Russian janitors: Eight voices simultaneously read eight different newspaper notices and get so hopelessly mixed up that not a phrase or a word can be understood in that chaos, try as one would.

The opera was based on the famous story of that name by N. Gogol, but missed its humorous realism and strayed to the realm of the anecdote. The very construction of the libretto (by J. Preis) is formalistic. The text was montaged from various stories by Gogol. Aside from the "Nose" story the opera contains excerpts from "Old Time Landowners," "Dead Souls," "Diary of a Madman," "Taras Bulba" and "The Wedding." In addition, the libretto possessed itself of Smerdyakov's little song from Dostoyevsky's "Brothers Karamazov." It is hardly necessary to so much as discuss such a method of dealing with classic literature. Obviously such a crazy-quilt libretto could not have furnished the composer with a real dramatic basis. To this was due the self-sufficiency of the music, as previously mentioned.

The opera "The Nose" told of the fantastic adventures

of Major Kovalev's nose which departed from its owner. One scene was more odd and unexpected than the other. The cast was large—numbering 70. With such a crowd on the stage individual characterization was out of the question of course. The characters frequently appeared merely to sing one or two phrases.

When writing "The Nose," the composer apparently forgot all the specifications of opera. This was evidenced first by the arrangement of the arias. The melodic principle in the usual sense was absent here. Recitative at times dwindled to ordinary speech. Shostakovich's recitative, moreover, was based on curious, onomatopoeic and exaggerated intonations. The vocal arrangement (and therefore the style of the entire opera) was marked by studied unnaturalness and downright burlesque. According to the author's note, for example, the aria of the Nose is to be sung nasally, while in the part of Major Kovalev there are vocalizations of consonant sounds, etc.

The orchestra unquestionably dominates this curious composition. The composer's ingenuity knows no bounds. From a limited number of instruments ("The Nose" bears the character of chamber music and employs no more than one representative of each type of instrument) he derives the most astonishing effects. All sorts of sounds are simulated by this curious orchestra: The clatter of horses' hoofs is rendered by a combination of the celesta and timpani, the hiccough of a drunkard, by harp, violin, and woodwind, the scraping of Major Kovalev's face with a razor, by piccolo and doublebass. The score abounds in such simulations and instrumental tricks.

In the opera too there are many independent instrumental episodes. Foremost among these are the entr'actes embodying the new constructive principles of Shostako-vich. Most characteristic was the entr'acte of the second scene written for timpani alone. This music, resembling that produced with combs, pails, bottles, etc., was stripped even of melody and harmony.

It goes without saying that no realistic presentation of characters was feasible. This seemed to have troubled the composer not at all. His attention, apparently, had been en-tirely absorbed by his search for new polyphonic effects. The swift song and dance patterns were executed by "masks" alone, each exaggerated to the point of absurdity.

Based on extreme naturalistic principles, this opera failed to survive as a musical and dramatic entity.

"The Nose" was staged in the Leningrad Maly Opera House on January 12, 1930. It was not produced anywhere else.

In Shostakovich's musical biography one may set down "The Nose" as a composition prompted by a mischievous and mocking spirit. With the spontaneity of youth the composer had engrossed himself in the element of musical grotesquery and burlesque.

"The Nose" is connected with certain tendencies of Soviet art in the Twenties. There was a time when the formalistic tendencies were quite strong in Soviet art and these in fact were responsible for the naturalistic erring of Shostakovich, for the "nonobjective paintings," for much of the ugly box-kite architecture and numerous theatrical performances which sacrificed realism and psychological conviction—these precious qualities of the Russian theatre —for deliberate unnaturalness, for the attainment of coarse external effects and scenic tricks. It is, of course, impossible completely to identify and define such phenomena. Each had its own peculiarities, but all, unquestionably, had common traits. At one time fanfared, the system of biomechanics exercised strong influence upon the music of Shostakovich. The influence of the formalistic theatre told not only in his treatment of the operatic genre, but in the very construction of the libretto with its principle of stringing together various works of different character. Similar methods of "editing" the classics were frequently applied on the stages of some theatres at the time.

The abstract eccentricity of "The Nose" left no tangible trace in the Soviet music theatres. It was a fortuitous and transient phenomenon. Though other compositions based on similar principles appeared at the same time, not one of them reached the naturalistic extremes of Shostakovich's opera. In such operas as "The Northern Wind" by L. Knipper or "Ice and Steel" by V. Deshevov the formalism of the music was combined with the attempt to lend expression to the themes of revolution. This distinguished them from Shostakovich's opera, which carried the formalistic method to its apex and thereby fully revealed its absurdity. The composer, apparently, realized this himself. In any case he returned no more to the principles of his first opera.

The opera was closely followed by two ballets: "The Golden Age" and "Bolt." Both were staged in the Leningrad Academic House of Opera and Ballet,[1] but were indifferently received by the public and were soon stricken from the repertory. The symphonic suite which evolved from the music of the ballet, however, was rendered at

[1] The premiere of "Golden Age" was held on October 27, 1930. "Bolt" was staged for the first time on April 8, 1931. Both were presented under the baton of Alexander Gauk.

numerous concerts and earned the young composer fresh renown as a musical satirist.

Some years later Shostakovich wrote the following about his first ballets: ". . . 'Golden Age' and 'Bolt,' it seems to me, were utterly unsuccessful from the point of view of the drama. I believe the principal mistake here was that the choreographers, while trying to reflect something of our days, completely ignored the specific requirements of the ballet. . . ." This was very true. The mediocre librettos were one of the principal reasons for the failure of the ballets. They prevented the composer from creating an organic, choreographic-musical entity. As a result both ballets were nothing more than a loose series of dances.

The action of "Golden Age" was laid in a big city during a world exhibition. It was the story of a Soviet football team abroad. Music hall scenes alternated with those of a stadium. There was a rather naive exposition of the great city's stratagems to divert the team. Essentially this work was more like a "revue" than a ballet.

The music of his first ballet was marked by the composer's brilliant gift for orchestration. In character it was quite different from that of his opera "The Nose"; the orchestra was very large and augmented by saxophones, accordions, a banjo and a number of brass instruments. Characteristic was the Adagio in the first act based on alternating solos of the saxophone, violin, baritone, clarinet and flutes. An example of the composer's skill was the "Polka," obviously written under the influence of Stravinsky's "Little Suite," though sharper and more paradoxical.[2]

[2] The "Polka" has been published in the author's pianoforte transcription. Shostakovich plays it often at concerts and it is invariably well received. It has achieved great popularity on programs abroad.

The subject matter of his second ballet, "Bolt," differed considerably from that of his first and was actually an exposure of stagnant petty bourgeois life. Here too the awkward and helpless libretto frustrated the hopes of the composer. The nature of the music was much like that of the first ballet. Orchestration here too predominated. For the variety of its effects this score surpassed everything hitherto written by the composer. When rendered in concert form the music of "The Bolt" amazes the listener by the fancifulness of its orchestration and the novelty of its effects. According to the composer the grotesque interrelation of melodies, upon which the ballet is built up, was to have achieved the purpose of satirizing the Philistine. Unfortunately he did not always display sufficient discrimination in his choice of melodies and the score therefore contained much that was banal. Such things as this threatened to sully Shostakovich's musical language. He was quick to realize it and in the future refrained from such risky experiments.

The ballets revealed the composer's strivings to create light and entertaining music. He admitted this himself: ". . . I hoped to write good entertaining music which would be pleasant or even amusing. . . . It gives me pleasure to see my audience laugh or at least smile." It is possible that this desire to amuse was the most valuable aspect of Shostakovich's work belonging to the years of his formalistic probings. The undeniable artistic value of his work is of less importance in this connection (though then too he brought forth veritable masterpieces such as his orchestration of Vincent Youmans' "Tahiti Trot" [3]) than the fact that he displayed initiative in this field at a time

[3] Some years later he wrote two splendid suites for jazz orchestras, much in the same spirit.

when some Puritans of music were ready to prohibit the lighter genres, regarding them as heinous sins. Outstanding musicians to this day tend to ignore the lighter genres. It is time that the latter took their rightful place in the sphere of symphonic music. Light, humorous and entertaining music must be included on the programs of the symphony orchestras. This was emphasized by Dmitri Shostakovich when he said: "I have yet to hear someone say that our Soviet symphony should simply entertain its listeners and this, by the way, is a problem which cannot be ignored." The composer is right. Entertaining, light genres can exist side by side with the profound and the heroic in symphonic programs.

Shostakovich continued to work in the sphere of the symphony. His Second and Third Symphonies treat with the theme of revolution. The Second Symphony, or "Symphonic Dedication to October," was written for the tenth anniversary of the Soviet State (1927). His Third, "May First," Symphony appeared in 1930. He was unable completely to master his themes however; the discrepancy between his ideas and means of expression was too great. Dealing with his new theme of revolution, he attempted to apply his universal, as they seemed to him, methods of modern technique.

"Symphonic Dedication to October" is a one-part composition for orchestra and chorus (the latter was written to the text of Alexander Bezymensky). As the first critics of the symphony observed, the composer attempted to depict the evolution of a guiding force and will from a state of initial chaos. The revolutionary theme was here handled as something cosmic. A comparison of this score with that of the First Symphony reveals the great changes that had

27

already taken place in the composer's consciousness. The well-defined images and clarity of construction in the earlier work had been superseded by the abstractions of individual fragments only superficially interwoven.

Here there was not a single, clear melodic form. The polyphony was woven from characterless melodies serving merely as constructional materials. The emotional principle was almost lacking. Vague symbolism was combined with the formal rationalism which gave rise to it. This is particularly apparent in the principal musical ideas of the symphony.

The beginning might almost be described as sheer noise. One by one melodic lines take shape but they are not connected either harmonically or thematically. Each runs its own course. The basic rhythms grow more and more intricate. The strings are joined by the brass and finally there emerges a new and more definite theme carried by a muted trumpet.

This subject evolving from the initial chaos is developed continuously without interruption. Automatism permeates the music. Its complex polyphonic culminations recall the "horizontal counterpoint" of Darius Milhaud. The combination of utterly alien melodies startles and attracts the eye, but no more than the eye, since it is more than doubtful that the human ear could comprehend anything in that chaos of tones. There is not even a trace of symphonic development; instead, there is a mechanical increment of individual voices culminating in precipitous chromatic scales. The sound is extremely harsh. Minor seconds leaping through nearly entire octaves tear the ear like a saw.

The imperious phrases of the horns are followed by a final chorus differing sharply from all that goes before.

The chorus derives its merit from its dynamic character and well-defined melody. It fails, however, to create the impression of a logical musical conclusion anticipated by the preceding development of the Finale, and appears to be merely a formal termination of the symphony.

The "May First" Symphony is simpler and clearer. The modulation here is developed far more logically; there is less harshness and confusion. Although the constructive principle is mainly linear, the individual polyphonic currents are very expressive. The main difference between this work and its predecessor is its determinate character. Entire passages are carried by genres expressive of national festivity (triumphal marches and stirring mass songs). The music therefore is more convincing and vital than that of the Second Symphony. The composer here too failed to free himself from his abstractions, to evolve an organic musical entity. The individual passages are merely assembled, but not welded together by the logic of sequential polyphonic ideas.

And yet, the composer's ideas were both daring and interesting. The Soviet music critic Boris Assafyev aptly observed that "this was practically the only attempt to launch a symphony on the oratory of revolution, on an atmosphere and intonations both oratorical." The oratorical principle, however, was set forth as something decorative, as though the composer was interested neither in the content of this oratory (not articulated oratory, impossible within the framework of a symphony, but the emotions attending stirring human speech), nor in the pathos of national festivity, but in its external manifestations—its gestures and its movement. Oratorical pathos therefore was superseded by rhetoric, just as the vital imagery was superseded by an externally symbolic parade to the drub of the Young Pioneers' Drums.

The reasons for the composer's failure in his Second and Third Symphonies were identical. First, the composers of the time were unable artistically to resolve the theme of revolution. The second reason lay in the character of the young composer who had not yet acquired sufficient experience to deal with so important a problem. Hence the deliberation with which he approached his subject and the application of methods incompatible with the content. The discrepancy between his ideas and means of expression was so great that neither his good will nor earnest efforts could save the situation. This accounts for the difference in the objective-historical and subjective-biographical significance of his Second and Third Symphonies. Such as they were, however, they represented an important phase in the composer's development, marked his approach to the profounder problems of his time and his striving to emerge from the narrow confines of "modernistic" esthetics. At the same time they bore witness to an acute creative crisis.

Shostakovich was trying to bring his art closer to the demands of life. This was indicated by his intensive efforts on behalf of the theatre and cinema. He had never been of an academic turn of mind, one who moved securely and snugly within the framework of conventional traditions. He was pleased to do his level best when creating so-called background music and here too did not stint his talent, ingenuity and skill.

Beginning with 1927 Shostakovich worked for various theatres in Leningrad and Moscow. Particularly extensive were his connections with the Young Workers' Theatre of Leningrad. All the actors of this theatre were workers who continued on the job in their respective plants and factories. They would spend the first half of the day at the work bench and the second half rehearsing in a hall of the theatre or on the stage. According to the founders of the theatre, this combination of factory work and acting was to promote a new scenic art. In this remarkable playhouse Shostakovich grew intimately acquainted with the young workers. Directing the theatre's musical activities, he also participated in the production of all of its plays and shows. A wide range of activity opened before him here since the performances were abundantly accompanied by music. His work in the theatre sharpened the composer's vision, augmented his skill in the composition of brief and clearly defined musical passages. His work on such plays as "The Shot," "Virgin Soil," "Rule Britannia" and others enabled him more closely to approach the new themes of Soviet life. All this, unquestionably, contributed to his development. His work in this theatre, however, may also have had a detrimental effect. Certain mechanistic principles and naturalistic tendencies of the theatre probably exercised no little influence.

These tendencies may have affected the composer even more during his work with other theatres. The once well-known system of scenic biomechanics, then prevalent in the theatres, undoubtedly had a telling effect. As previously mentioned, the principles of biomechanics influenced the opera "The Nose." This did not escape the attention of discerning musicians. Boris Assafyev, for example, wrote: ". . . It would not be at all paradoxical to say that to sense the proportions of Shostakovich's music one requires not the time for mental assimilation, for emotion mentally evoked (the time to "feel"), but the time necessary for a gesture, a reflex movement, one might say for the 'intonation' of the body. That is why his music seems to be permeated with peculiar gesticulation, actions." All this fits in with the principles of biomechanics. It likewise denied the necessity of emotional assimilation and evolved from the external gesture and movement, regarding this as the alpha and omega of the actor's skill. Renunciation of the emotional and psychological is a similar phenomenon in, and characteristic of, certain works of Shostakovich.

Another detrimental tendency of the theatre which had its effect on Shostakovich was its arbitrary interpretation and "renovation" of the classics. Realism and historic truth were sacrificed to the unprincipled imagination of the regisseur. We may cite the operas "The Nose" and "Catherine Izmailova," for instance. These works of two great Russian writers received a "new," but essentially distorted, interpretation. The same was true of the music to "Hamlet," as produced by the Moscow Vakhtangov Theatre. Despite its bright moments and original conception, the score to "Hamlet" was as questionable as the production with which it was so closely bound.

Though taking into account the negative phenomena of theatrical art in those years, it would not do to underestimate the importance of Shostakovich's work for the theatre. More fruitful and successful, however, was his work for the cinema.

His first contact with the cinema was the music he wrote for the silent film "New Babylon." It was supposed to have been played with the film in Leningrad, but as it so happened it was not used. In one of Moscow's cinemas, however, it was repeatedly rendered by a symphony orchestra under the baton of F. Krish.

From the first day of the talkies Shostakovich became

a faithful devotee of the new art. Very quickly he found a common language with the cinema folk, who came to regard him as one of themselves on the movie lots. From the outset, he was connected with such masters of the Soviet cinema as Ermler, Kozintsev and Trauberg and shared their enthusiasm over the new genre, the film. His ties with the cinema are equally close today.

Outstanding among his early works in this field was the music of the films "Alone," "Golden Hills" and "Counterplan." So broadly conceived was the music to "Golden Hills" that the composer subsequently used it for an interesting concert suite. The individual parts of the suite—the subtly conventionalized old waltz, the dynamic fugue and intermezzo, the pathetic funeral march—are fine symphonic passages, each valuable in its own right. At the same time they harmonized well with the film, intensifying and emphasizing the scenes. Shostakovich here showed how "background" music should be treated to maintain the continuity of the film and yet preserve its own value as something original and independent. Equally successful was his music to the film "Counterplan." The basic passage here was a buoyant, melodic song which was eagerly caught up by the Soviet youth throughout the country. (The song from "Counterplan" was published in the United States in 1942 with new words by Harold Rome—"United Nations.") Some years later Shostakovich wrote the music for a number of popular Soviet films. It was he who wrote the music to the film trilogy about Maxim (great popularity accrued to his handling of an old urban ditty in this film), to the "Great Citizen," "Man with the Gun," "Lenin in October" and others. In cinema music Shostakovich at once found the right path, and his contributions in this sphere have added much to Soviet art.

The composer himself was not satisfied with his work for the cinema. He sought for greater freedom of expression and tried more persistently to introduce the symphonic principles to the cinema. He was also far from satisfied with the technical aspects; his highly sensitive ear craved supreme purity of sound, flexibility and faultless precision even in the most subtle of polyphonic nuances. He began to dream of a greater cinema art, of a new genre of cinema opera. His plans engrossed him. He meant to avail himself of cinema potential for the creation of a dynamic opera pervaded with action. No doubt, he could have succeeded in this. There is an affinity between the swift flow of his music and the dynamic principle of cinema art. Both throb to the pulse of modern times and both are full of action. This, perhaps, was the reason why he took so easily to the genre of "background" music.

*   *   *

Two conflicting tendencies mark Shostakovich's work in the period between 1927–1932. The first was to assimilate various currents of modern western music, a tendency which consecutively found expression in his opera "The Nose," a sonata and "Aphorisms" for the pianoforte. The second, no less pronounced, was his search for new themes closely allied to Soviet reality. This gave rise to his Second and Third Symphonies and his "background" music for the theatre and cinema. Naturally, these contrary tendencies lent a contradictory nature to his work.[4] Markedly unstable in those years, his music was ever probing for the new, ever

[4] These tendencies naturally do not always appear disassociated from one another, but are often interwoven in the most weird and complex fashion (Second Symphony).

34

undergoing experimentation, ever drifting from sphere to sphere. The composer undoubtedly was progressing, but slowly and painfully.

Shostakovich proved able to assimilate the various influences and very soon evolved his own style. His development in those years was mainly evidenced by his growing mastery of music, a mastery, as it seemed to him (and many others) which was universal and applicable to all themes. In reality, it was most specific and limited. Whenever he attempted to deal with new problems with the means at his command he invariably found himself in deep water. His customary methods proved insufficient and he had to find new principles of expression. He had yet to meet with many temptations and find the strength to overcome them. One of these was his infatuation with unemotional constructivism and his weakness for reckless eccentricities. Another—apparently contrary, but actually related to the first—was his penchant for naturalism and expressionism. His creative crisis grew, was aggravated steadily until it reached its culminating point in the opera "Lady Macbeth of Mtsensk (Catherine Izmailova)." A gifted work, though full of glaring discrepancies, this opera revealed the composer's progress and his earnest effort to deal with realistic and pertinent subjects.

35

CHAPTER III

CRISIS

Sнostakovich worked over his opera "Lady Macbeth of Mtsensk" for two years (1930–1932). Impatiently awaited by the public, it gripped the attention of the musical world. Probably no other work of his pen grew to be the object of such heated discussion. From the start it evoked varied and often contradictory comment. Aside from the composer's admirers who regarded this work as a new dawn in the resurrection of opera, there were a number of musicians who criticized it in no uncertain terms. Equally varied were the opinions of the wider circles of concert goers. The opera was produced both in the U.S.S.R. (by the Leningrad Maly Academic Theatre, the Nemirovich-Danchenko Theatre and State Academic Bolshoi Opera House) and abroad, in the cities of New York, Cleveland, London, Prague, Zurich, Stockholm, etc.[1]

Particularly heated were the discussions about this opera

[1] The premiere of "Lady Macbeth of Mtsensk" was staged by the Leningrad Maly Opera House under the baton of S. Samosud on January 22, 1934. Somewhat later it was produced by the Nemirovich-Danchenko Theatre. Both productions were on a high level. Soviet opera stars once more demonstrated their ability to cope with the difficulties of Shostakovich's vocal music. Especially striking were the settings of the Nemirovich-Danchenko Theatre which tempered much that was grossly extreme and naturalistic.

in the U.S.S.R., after a number of articles on the subject appeared in the newspaper "Pravda" in January 1936.

The opera "Lady Macbeth of Mtsensk" was based on a story of the same title by that fine Russian author Nikolai Leskov whose works are so remarkable for their colour, freshness and richness of language (this was noted by Maxim Gorky who regarded Leskov as "an unsurpassed master of the Russian language"). In his novel "Lady Macbeth of Mtsensk" Leskov depicted the life of the merchants in the provinces, their boorishness and cruelty.

The opera in brief is as follows: Zinovi Izmailov, son of a wealthy merchant, marries the poor girl Catherine. She does not love her husband, and is dismally bored by her idle mode of life. The master of the house is her domineering and harsh old father-in-law Boris Timofeyevich, who jealously watches over the order of his house and forces all to comply with his will. The Izmailovs hire a new clerk, the handsome, impudent Sergei with the reputation of a Don Juan. He becomes the lover of Catherine. Returning from a tryst one night, Sergei is intercepted by Izmailov Senior. Punishment is swift. By order of the master the servants flog Sergei and lock him up in the cold barn. To avenge her lover Catherine decides to poison her father-in-law, Boris Timofeyevich. The crime binds her more firmly to Sergei and she conceives the idea of ridding herself of her disagreeable husband, of seizing possession of the rich merchant's house and making Sergei her lawful husband. These plans are put to action. With Sergei's help she murders Zinovi and walls up the corpse in the cellar. Nothing is left to hamper the lovers. They arrange a sumptuous wedding. At the height of the merry-making one of the servants accidentally discovers Zinovi's corpse and at once reports to the police. Catherine and Sergei are arrested, tried, and sentenced to hard labor in Siberia.

With a detachment of convicts Sergei and Catherine trudge along a wide Siberian highway. Sergei is filled with rage and hatred. Surfeited with Catherine, he can only regard her as the authoress of his misfortune, but she loves him as ardently as before. The denouement is sudden. Sergei transfers his affections to the young convict Sonetka. Mad with grief, Catherine pushes her rival into a river and she too is drowned. The convicts trudge wearily on, toward their dismal destination.

There are three scenes in the First Act. The first deals nearly entirely with Catherine: her solitude, melancholy idleness, her purposeless existence are depicted by the music, penetratingly sensitive. The hearer's sympathy is won with the very first appearance of Catherine. The lyric charm of Catherine is in harsh contrast with those who surround her. The second half of the scene therefore is treated differently. Here there is the dry, rasping aria of Boris Timofeyevich (exaggerated conversational intonations), the sharp, over-boisterous chorus of the clerks, reminiscent of Shostakovich's cherished world of grotesquery. The music, though, is simpler and clearer than that of the opera "The Nose."

The second scene, depicting the humiliation of the working woman Aksinya, presents a veritable apotheosis of the boorishness and club-law which reigned supreme in the house of the Izmailovs. No little ingenuity was displayed by the composer in depicting in his music the gestures of the unbridled crowd of clerks. The music of this scene, cynical and coarse in its naturalism, clashes with the monologue of Catherine which displays new features of her character. Whereas her portrayal in the first scene was lyrical, she here represents a living protest against the humble status of womanhood. The simplicity and severity of this passage, the emotional intensity of its melody, as in the first scene, is contrasted with a tortuous chorus of guttural, monstrous images (the element of unemotional, mechanical movement once more dominates here).

Similar contrasts may be found in the third scene which opens with the musical recitative of Catherine. (Its accompanying rhythm lends it a palpitating, nervous nature.) This is followed by the beautiful song "Through the Window Today I Saw." One of the finest pages of the opera, it subtly resurrects the Russian popular song of the nineteenth century. The poetic charm, however, is effaced by the ensuing scene of Catherine and Sergei's meeting. Permeated with the rhythms of the polka and galop, this music runs the entire gamut of naturalism.

Two tendencies oppose each other in the First Act: the striving to create something that is human, vividly emotional, and the naturalistic portrayal of the sombre sides of old Russian life.

The Second Act smacks of the erotic and is pervaded by the spirit of criminal adventure. This pertains particularly to the scene with Boris Timofeyevich. The illicit longings of the sensual old man serve as a unique pendant to Catherine's aria which is evolved in an unexpectedly cynical manner. Features of the same coarse naturalism may be observed in the scenes of Sergei's punishment and of Boris Timofeyevich's death. In addition to these purely descriptive and caricatured passages predominating in the first scene (the clerk's chorus "A crocodile cruel our master is") there are several stirring and dramatic passages. Such is Catherine's lamentation over the corpse of Boris Timo-

39

feyevich. The composer here availed himself of the intonations of the professional Russian mourners of olden times [2] which here sound particularly ironic and acutely express the hypocrisy of Catherine lamenting the death of her father-in-law whom she has murdered.

The fifth scene is one of the strong moments of drama in the opera. There is the appearance of Boris Timofeyevich's ghost and the ominous monologue of Catherine: "Old Boris thought to interfere, and so died Boris." Another masterly scene is where Catherine and her lover wall up the corpse of Zinovi Borisovich in the cellar. The action unfolds against the background of a restrained march-like movement. Furtive wariness and alarm are expressed by the simplest and therefore most potent means.

Catherine now appears in a new light. Having committed double murder and buried the corpse of her husband in the cellar, she is at last able to marry Sergei and become full mistress of the house. Gone is her lyrical pining and pathos! Arrogance and unbridled sensuality come to the fore. There is something macabre in her repeated: "Kiss me, again!" This against a background of an ominous finale march.

---

[2] The genre of funeral lament was widely applied in Russian popular poetry and music. In olden days it was an invariable custom at funerals. In the villages and hamlets there were the so-called "wailers," women known for their skill at lamenting. Folk laments have been studied by Russian philologists and are as valuable in their way as other heritages of Russian folklore. Maxim Gorky described his impressions of the lamentation of the famous mourner Orinushka. He was "completely under the spell of these original, heart-rending laments, gripped by the melancholy and tearful melodies. The lament of the Russian woman bewailing her hard fate flowed from the dry lips of the poetess, and scourged the soul with its grief, its pain. . . ." The scene of Catherine's lament conforms to this tradition and introduces something truly realistic in the opera.

Parody is sharp in the Third Act and already appears in the drunken song of the "befuddled little sot." The recklessness of instrumentation here knows no bounds. There is one of those galloping rhythms typical of the composer and ludicrously accelerated by snatches of Russian popular song. The dynamics of the cinema pervade the entire scene from the drunken carousing to the sobering jolt which shakes the "befuddled little sot" when he chances upon the corpse hidden in the cellar.

The galloping rhythm continues through the symphonic entr'acte introducing the seventh scene, laid in a precinct police station. The spectator is confronted with the guardians of the law, the district police sergeant and his underlings. The composer found vivid means to depict their stupidity. The recitative of the sergeant is highly characteristic and so too the policemen's chorus, "For a tip or a bribe a ready crew," a rollicking waltz. The scene culminates in a new galop when the policemen headed by their officer hurry off to apprehend the miscreants. All this recalls the tension of the adventure film.

No less cinematographic is the eighth scene—a series of satirical sketches of the wedding celebration. In the foreground there are Catherine and Sergei. Anticipating calamity, they are nervous, uneasy and contemplating flight. But too late! They hear the footsteps of the police. Tragic are the final exclamations of Catherine. Faced by retribution, they lose their nerve and surrender themselves helplessly to justice.

The Fourth Act is the most integral and important in the opera. Many pages here were penned with a masterly hand. The story hitherto was devoted entirely to Catherine, but the composer now portrays the sorrow and suffering of the people. The monologue of the old convict and the convicts' chorus ("Weary way to bondage") are good examples. The music of the chorus is near to the traditions of Mussorgsky, but presents them in an entirely new way. Using the folk song intonation as his point of departure, Shostakovich found other conventional but unique means of expression as evidenced by their harmony, a combination of pure triads and subtle polytonality. Here too there is a noteworthy variation of the linear principles: the unexpected introduction of a subordinate *ostinato* movement into the broad flow of the principal melody of the chorus.

The composer's depiction of womanhood bowed under a weight of grief is truly convincing art. Catherine's monologues "After honour and praise—how hard to face the judge's frown" and "A lake in the heart of the forest" regain the sympathy of her hearers.

For all its merits the music of the Fourth Act also has its anomalies—such as the scene of Sergei and Sonetka. In content and musical language it has much in common with some of the lurid naturalistic passages in previous acts of the opera. Alongside of the moving choruses this music seems quite out of place.

The final pages of the opera—the death of Catherine and departure of the convicts—sound like a great lament, grief implacable and a curse on the hated past. The tragic characters presented by the composer in his music as clearly as they were shown on the stage indicated what he would be capable of, once free from his formalistic errings.

* * *

The composer's attention is focussed upon Catherine. This character is vividly and sympathetically presented. She is surrounded by masks that are hideous and evil—the weak-minded Zinovi Borisovich, the cruel and domineering Boris Timofeyevich, the scoundrelly Sergei, the loutish clerks and policemen. This contrast is well brought out by the music of the opera. Catherine's part is natural, genuine. All the others are expressed by music deliberately harsh and often chaotic. The idea of the composer is clear: Catherine is the only genuine person and is surrounded by brutes, libertines and pariahs. The composer himself did not hesitate to affirm this: ". . . I was out to justify Catherine in every way. I wanted the hearers and spectators to preserve a sympathetic impression of her. . . . I tried to present Catherine as a positive character, one who deserved the sympathy of the audience. Such sympathy was not easily evoked. Catherine is guilty of behavior that does not conform to the canons of ethics—she has committed a double murder. It is mainly here that there is a departure from Leskov's story. He described Catherine as a cruel woman, depraved. I refused to take such a course and presented her as a clever woman, gifted and interesting. Her nightmarish surroundings, the cruel and selfish routine of the merchant's house render her life dreary and very sad. She does not love her husband, knows no joy and no consolation. . . . It would be correct to say that her crimes represented a protest against the life which she was compelled to lead, against the sordid and stuffy atmosphere of the merchant milieu of the nineteenth century. The music was calculated to justify Catherine in every way, criminal though she was and, borrowing the words of Dobrolyubov, we might say that she 'was a ray of light in the kingdom of darkness.' Aside from Catherine there is no positive character or hero in this opera." [3]

[3] D. Shostakovich: "My Ideas about Lady Macbeth." Libretto of the opera, Moscow, 1935.

This statement of the composer reveals the idea behind the opera and the degree of its departure from the novel of Leskov. It would be wrong to condemn out of hand the very principle of 'revising' a literary text. The opera composer has the right to do this. As is known, many great operas of the past departed considerably from the stories upon which they were based. The fact that Shostakovich departed from Leskov's story is not as important as the idea which the story gained in its new version. It is scarcely necessary to point out the discrepancy between the composer's conception of the opera and historic reality. It is perfectly true that in the past the lot of the Russian woman was very hard. But even in such sordid surroundings as those of Catherine there were strong, honorable women, courageous and devoted.

As for Catherine, one may say that she herself is an outgrowth of that milieu against which Shostakovich had meant to pose her. Catherine does not suffer because she is superior to those who surround her. Had she accomplished her aim of marrying Sergei she too would have become a ruthless mistress. Her crimes do not at all represent a protest against the realities about her, and the measures taken to punish her are by no means a social tragedy.

Incorrect handling of the central theme is the chief shortcoming and is directly responsible for all the other weaknesses of the opera, its dualisms and contradictions. Closely interwoven in the opera are the realistic and naturalistic tendencies of the composer. To this too the music owes its eclectic character. Certain pages of the opera are undoubtedly of an original harmonic and melodic nature, but all too frequent are the unnatural twists of melody, studied illogical sequence of ideas and deliberate harshness of harmony. The problem of purity and unity of style had not yet been solved by the composer. Something similar may be observed in the libretto written by Y. Preis, which abounds in redundant nonsense and coarse expressions. The Russian language here is affectedly rendered as "plain," but actually is revoltingly low. Y. Preis perhaps had meant to parody the language used by the characters portrayed. In reality he distorted and mutilated the spirit of the Russian language in a crass, formalistic manner.

The subject matter of the opera called for extensive use of the Russian folk song. Unlike the music of the first opera, undistinguished in character, the finest pages of the second opera are rich in Russian folk melody. This is true primarily of many of Catherine's arias, some of which are not alien to the songs of the Russian peasant (the laments) and the song popular through the countryside of old Russia ("Today Through the Window I Saw"). There is a curious effect of poignance in the expressionist treatment of Russian song idioms in Catherine's final monologue. Even nearer to the traditions of Russian folk art is the music of the Fourth Act and particularly so the fine music of the convicts' chorus. Shostakovich here won for his music that moving quality and immense breadth once achieved by the great Mussorgsky himself.

The opera has considerable melodic variety, but declamatory tendencies predominate on the whole. The harmonic language too is anything but monotonous. Strict diatonism, curiously logical cadences and harmonic progressions are often intermixed with most abstruse-polytonal and even atonal patterns. There are times when the use of polytonal principles is artistically justified and represents a powerful means of expression in the hands of the composer. More

45

frequently it leads him into a jungle of harsh and distressing combinations of sound, into the realms of musical extravagance.

Shostakovich's orchestration displays the usual ingenuity. More often than not his probings are of a naturalistic character and abstract. This is especially evidenced in the orchestral entr'actes. Such are the harsh gallopades of the entr'actes to the third, seventh and eighth scenes. Other of his searchings recall the music of Alban Berg, as, for example, the symphonic entr'acte to the fifth scene—a broadly developed *passacaglia*.

An important role in the music of "Lady Macbeth" devolves upon mechanistic movement, often the basis of an entire large scene. This sometimes serves to emphasize the meaning as, for example, the chorus of clerks taking leave of Zinovi Borisovich. The mechanistic passage is admirably suited to the grotesque situation. At other times, however, it contradicts the meaning of the scene, anticipates or lags behind it (the scene of Zinovi Borisovich's departure).

Discrepancies between the text, the situation on the stage and the character of the music are frequent in the opera. Here, obviously, there is a connection with the esthetic principles of cinematography, particularly with the practice of asynchronization. In general, the influence of the cinema on modern music is very considerable. Many composers, since the invention of sound films, have been participating in the process of producing films. Music is playing an ever greater role in the cinema and at times becomes the chief component (Disney's animated cartoons, the "Great Waltz," "Alexander Nevsky" and others). The specifications of the new genre exercise great influence on musical composition as a whole. As for Shostakovich, who has done a good deal of work for the cinema, he has displayed a perfect understanding of the laws of this art and employed much of it in his operas and ballets. It was the cinema which prompted the swift development of action and the scene-by-scene construction. Again it was the cinema which prompted asynchronization of music and text. The latter method is by no means always happily applied by the composer. The asynchronous principle is transferred to the opera mechanically and acquires quite a different aspect. In the cinema an effect is often produced by the incongruity of the main—visual—imagery and its accompanying musical imagery. In the opera the musical imagery is the dominating element and more than anything else serves to create an impression. Asynchronism, therefore, very frequently distorts and alters the main idea.

As compared with his first opera, "Lady Macbeth" in many ways was a step forward. It contains elements of realism, integral and convincing dramatic episodes. Several of the individual scenes are artistically true and written with a masterly touch. Intrinsic contradictions, however, were responsible for many serious shortcomings of the composer. The opera "Lady Macbeth" was a warning of the danger that menaced Shostakovich's development as a composer and also of a harmful deviation existing in Soviet art as a whole. That the composer was so gifted merely aggravated this danger. The younger composers were beginning to draw certain conclusions from Shostakovich's experience with musical drama.

But before we reach the turning point in Shostakovich's career, it is necessary to mention his ballet "Bright Rivulet," which appeared soon after "Lady Macbeth" and also, though somewhat differently, reflected his crisis. "Bright Rivulet" [4] deals with a modern theme. The action is laid on a Kuban collective farm and treats of the amusing adventures of a troupe of artists visiting the collective farmers. The author had meant to present a festive sort of a show, a scene of happy collective farm life. Owing to the superficial treatment of the theme, however, something quite different evolved. An ambiguous sort of a work, it contained nothing (except for acrobatic dances) to distinguish it from numerous other pieces on the subject of "country life." The libretto and the production as a whole therefore proved utterly trivial and false.

The music, unfortunately, failed to rise above the shortcomings of the libretto. The composer had believed that the music of "Bright Rivulet" was "cheerful, light, entertaining and, most important, suitable for the dance." He spoke of his attempts "here to find a musical language that was simple and accessible to spectators and performers alike." [5] Actually, his music turned out to be superficial and flippant. As B. Assafyev aptly observed: "striving to unfold the subject matter of the collective farm he solved his problem by borrowing a page from the lexicon of vaudeville, *i.e.*, 'lumpenmusik.' " [6] Failing to tap the rich music of the Cossack dances, the composer deprived his ballet of local color. Stitched into the score of the "collective farm" ballet were excerpts from his "industrial" ballet, "Bolt." All this curiously contradicted the composer's assertion that

[4] The ballet was composed in 1934 and first produced at the Leningrad Theatre of Opera and Ballet on April 4, 1935.
[5] Shostakovich: "My Third Ballet." "Bright Rivulet," Collected Material, Leningrad, 1935.
[6] B. Assafyev: "Troubling Questions," Soviet Music, No. 3, 1936. "Lumpenmusik," German term, meaning music for the useless, insincere.

Soviet themes for the ballet required a very serious approach.

The ballet contains not a hint of real life on the collective farms. Though simpler and more clear, the music recalls the grotesqueries of the first two ballets.

The article, "A Muddle in Lieu of Music," published in the newspaper "Pravda" on January 26, 1936, severely criticized Shostakovich's "Lady Macbeth." "From the outset," wrote the "Pravda," "the listeners were stunned by that deliberate and ugly flood of confusing sound. Shreds of melody and choking phrases of music were drowned out, burst forth to vanish again in a pandemonium of creaking, shrieking and crashes. It is difficult to follow such 'music' and utterly impossible to remember it. This went on nearly throughout the opera. On the stage the singing was superseded by bawling. When the composer accidentally struck a simple, tuneful melody he seemed to shrink away from it as from a calamity and to hurl himself with renewed fury into a jungle of confusing sound, in places pure and unadulterated cacophony. Expression for which the hearer craves is replaced by mad rhythm. This noisy music is supposed to express passion." The article did not deny the talent of the composer and was not directed against the work as a whole: "This is neither due to want of talent on the part of the composer nor to his inability to express simple and stirring sentiments. This music was deliberately turned 'topsy turvy' so that it should not remind one of classical opera, so that it should have nothing in common with customary symphonic music, with plain music comprehensible to all. Denying the principles of opera this music was based on those principles according to which ultra-left art as a whole denies the theatre simplicity; realism, comprehensibility and the natural meaning of words. . . . The danger of such a tendency in Soviet music is obvious. The ultra-left distortions in opera have their rise from the same sources as they have in painting, poetry, pedagogics and science." The article posed the timely question of combatting the formalistic tendencies so alien to the spirit of Soviet art and so remote from the realistic heritages of the great masters.

Reviewing the ballet "Bright Rivulet," "Pravda" in its article "Ballet Fallacy" criticized the superficiality of both the libretto and the music: ". . . The ballet is one of our most conservative forms of art and finds it more difficult than any other to break with those traditions which shaped the tastes of the pre-revolutionary audiences. The oldest of these traditions is that of the doll-like, unreal attitude toward life. Ballets prompted by such tendencies do not portray people, but dolls, creatures that are moved by the 'sentiments' of dolls. The basic difficulty of Soviet ballet is the fact that dolls are here impossible. Their falsity would be glaring and unbearable. This imposes serious obligations on the author of the ballet, the producers and the theatre as a whole. . . . The life of the collective farm, its new customs as yet in the process of formation are significant and most important subjects which must not be handled lightmindedly and without sufficient knowledge, be it in drama, opera or ballet. . . ."

Subsequent events fully justified these criticisms of "Pravda." Soviet art grew strong in its struggle against formalism and achieved a number of outstanding successes. The criticisms of "Pravda" were also justified by the works of Shostakovich whose gifts fully unfolded only when he had surmounted the follies of formalism.

Before dealing with the mature work of the composer it is necessary to mention certain of his works which appeared nearly simultaneously with "Lady Macbeth" and which clearly indicated his tendencies to break with formalism. These compositions signified a change in his style and voiced ideas and emotional motifs that were new to him. This applies to his Pianoforte Concerto, his preludes for the pianoforte and Violoncello Sonata, all of which were of a transitional character. The fallacies of his old work are observable here still, but ever clearer one may discern the outlines of his new style indicating that the process of his struggle against formalistic tendencies had been steady though slow. The articles of "Pravda," therefore, did not serve as the external impulse which changed his art, but rather accelerated that process which had already begun in the depths of his consciousness.

* * *

The Pianoforte Concerto is the largest work written for that instrument by the composer. This composition is curious for its unique reflection of the traditions of Russian pianoforte concertos and—at the same time—for its dissimilarity with the latter. Its chamber music character—the piano is accompanied by solo trumpet and string quintet—reminds one of the old pre-classical instrumental concerto. To some extent this is related to the neoclassicism of the pianoforte concertos of Hindemith and Poulenc. But in Shostakovich's case the old traditions are enriched by those of Russian music and therefore bear an entirely different character.

In his concerto Shostakovich denies the romantic school of piano composition and somewhat approaches the pianism of Prokofieff's early works. Renouncing the full register potential of the instrument, the technique of resounding chords and the rich pedal effects, he wove a piano pattern that was laconic, as subtly graphic as filigree work, and bare of pianistic frills. This also displayed Shostakovich's style of piano playing to best advantage. No one can render his piano compositions with more precision and clarity than he. One may perhaps complain of this precision which at times seems unduly dry. One may perhaps blame him for his redundant rationalism, but one cannot help sense the conviction carried by his composition. Dynamic and impulsive, it is yet guided by a strong and orderly will.

When comparing this concerto with his preceding works one notices a distinct clarification in his pianistic eloquence, more genuine and emotional than hitherto. Certain critics were inclined to complain of the concerto's levity, pointing to the second theme of the first part and the galloping Finale. This is hardly just. The composition contains much that is earnest and penetrating. Evolving dramatically, it proceeds from its tense introductory themes to a fiery finale. The scherzo-like passages served as a contrast and in their nature are not alien to the instrumental concerto.

The main theme of the first part is earnest in character and severe in outline. Its broad, unhurried evolution reminds one of Rachmaninov. The pathetic, declamatory nature of subsequent passages departs considerably from the grave and impressive introduction.

The transition to the second theme is very brief—two bars. This serves to emphasize the contrast. The second theme, lively and very mobile, is carried with grace and ease by the trumpet.

The second part of the concerto is a languid and not unpoetic waltz movement. The broad, melodic outline is permeated with tender lyricism and loses none of its continuity even during sudden tonal alterations. The element of contrast, reminiscent of the pathetic first part, is here discerned only in the central passage. All the more pacifying is the conclusion wherein the main theme is melodiously carried by a violoncello.

The brief third movement is a transition to the finale. Calm and unruffled, it is of a meditative nature and tinged with that severity which reminds one of the main theme of the first movement.

The finale is vivid and lithe. Its varied themes, sudden changes of passages and impulsive rhythms lend it a precipitous character, demonstrating Shostakovich's penchant for the scherzo. There is much here to remind the listener of conventional, modern grotesquerie, but he will find neither its extravagance nor dry constructivism.

*   *   *

The composer's twenty-four preludes for the pianoforte, written in the period from December 1932 to March 1933, were never properly evaluated. At first they were overshadowed by "Lady Macbeth." Later they were consigned to the shelves of Shostakovich's formalistic works. As a matter of fact these compositions, though of unequal value, played an important part in his development. The prelude traditions of Bach and Chopin found fertile soil for their development in Russian pianoforte music. This is sufficiently evidenced by the cycles of pianoforte compositions written by Scriabin (a continuer of Chopin) and Rachmaninov. The pianoforte music of the West during the second half of the nineteenth century and the first part of the present century underwent no similar evolution. The only important cycle of preludes written by Debussy was composed in an entirely different manner (Debussy's preludes comprise a series of impressionistic sketches and not psychological reflections as the preludes of Chopin). Shostakovich continued directly along the path of Chopin-Scriabin-Rachmaninov. He conceived of his preludes as a series of psychological sketches and this brought him close to the traditions of Russian pianoforte composition.

The importance of the preludes for Shostakovich lies in their emotional significance. Though he failed to attain the wealth of emotion of the unsurpassed preludes of Chopin, he nonetheless touched upon much that was hitherto beyond his creative horizon. His means of expression here are incomparably more clear than they were in his early pianoforte compositions. What the preludes lacked, however, was unity of style. The melodies fluctuated from the sublime to the downright banal. The genres were widely varied—from the exacting Fugato (E-minor prelude) to the lithe "Velocity Etude" (D-major prelude with scale passages reminiscent of Czerny's "School of Velocity").

Outstanding among the others is the sombre and tragic E-flat minor prelude. A melody arising from the lower register breaks through to the highest register like a cry of pain. The lyricism of this prelude reveals new features of Shostakovich's talent subsequently expressed in the grave movements of his symphonies. In severity of outline this prelude calls to mind the lofty portals of a Gothic church. Leopold Stokowski transcribed it for the symphony orchestra and rendered it many times at various concerts.

The last of the twenty-four is the D-minor prelude, a

54

grotesque tangent of the popular dance genre. It is not difficult to observe its ties with jazz. It ends, however, in an unexpected reflective vein. This epilogue prelude contrasts sharply with the pathetic conclusions of the Chopin and Scriabin preludes.

*　　*　　*

In 1934 Shostakovich wrote a sonata for violoncello and pianoforte. This new venture into chamber music differed greatly from his string octet by its more significant content and emotion. Like the Pianoforte Concerto and the preludes, the Violoncello Sonata belongs to the transitionary period in the art of the composer.

The first movement owes its merit to its remarkable themes. The first is elegiac and serene, the second somewhat brighter and warmed by lyric emotion. Unfortunately, melodic clarity here is at times dimmed by redundant complexity.

The final pages of the first movement are the finest. The main theme is sounded against a restrained passage of the pianoforte. It tapers gradually to melancholy minor thirds. Dull strokes of the basses complete the passage. All this anticipates the coda of the first movement of the Fifth Symphony.

The second part, a waltz, is somewhat mechanical in movement and lacks the simplicity of the best scherzos of Shostakovich. The mechanical effect is heightened by the absence of vivid melodic phrases. The vitality of the Scherzo in the Fifth Symphony or of the Pianoforte Quintet is yet lacking.

The third movement—Largo—is drawn in sombre colors, hopelessly sad. Here there is much warmth of feeling, rarely weakened by certain abstractions. Particularly fine is the sonorous main theme.

The finale—with its subtle humor, scintillating melody and crisp gait—is exceedingly attractive. The resounding first theme, the precipitous passages of the pianoforte and the great charm of the final pages where the pianoforte theme is accompanied by a violoncello pizzicato invariably captivates the audience.

Our review of the most complex and contradictory phase in the creative evolution of Shostakovich concludes at this point. The composer has risen to the level of a master, and, having overcome many detrimental tendencies, has forged his own mature and original style. In his development, one may say, the pendulum swung to the extreme left where he found himself in the grip of unemotional, constructivist principles. But persevering through the maze of his own and others' errors he found his own, independent style at last. Not only has he stood all trials, but even in his errors he remained an outstanding composer, quite different from others attempting to wield "unusual means of expression." The power of his musical intellect was shown in many ways—in his phenomenal facility of composition, his independent manner of dealing with various influences and the variety of tasks which he set himself.

Shostakovich has bewitched many by his masterly treatment of musical material inaccessible to others, and the artistic failings of some of his works at times escaped general notice. To justify mistakes on the score of talent and ingenuity of technique is an extremely dangerous matter. It might lead one to the conclusion that sheer technique is the chief thing. Styles that are not his own are bound to insinuate themselves into the mind of the artist, and woe to

56

him who is lured astray by the superficial novelty of certain technical methods and to these sacrifices the sacred truths of art. One might say that the extent of the artist's mistakes will be proportionate to his talent, and the greater his gifts the greater will have to be the efforts which he must expend to regain the highroad of art. For this reason academic complacence is out of place when estimating the formalistic errors of a composer, and, particularly, of so gifted a composer as Dmitri Shostakovich.

Now that the old controversies have been settled it is possible to review objectively the evolution of the composer. The errors of many of his former tendencies are now obvious and much that was once regarded as significant has faded. On the other hand, it appears that much of his work was unjustly forgotten and deserves better appraisal than it ever received. Such works as the pianoforte preludes and concerto, the violoncello sonata, the symphonic suite of "Golden Hills," "Hamlet" and others were milestones in the history of Soviet music and have preserved their value to this day. The best of the composer's works at that time anticipated the means of expression which he was subsequently to unfold in his symphonic and instrumental masterpieces. These works, in fact, have reflected the growth of Soviet music which has earned not a few successes in the past years.

A proper understanding of this phase of the composer's development will lead to the realization that he has attained maturity, that he has surmounted and discarded the heritage of formalism. His Pianoforte Quintet, the Fifth and the Seventh Symphonies were evolved after he had run the gauntlet of harrowing doubts and disappointments.

A salient feature of the composer's progress was the

57

fact that his efforts to pursue the positive traditions of his art were steadily intensified as the period of creative crisis grew upon him. There was something contradictory therefore in the very evolution of his talent. Deep in his consciousness he was constantly waging an implacable though hidden struggle for the attainment of a new style.

CHAPTER IV

WINNING FREE!

MORE QUICKLY than other musicians Shostakovich understood the essence of the severe criticisms levelled against him. An honest artist and truthful to the core, he did not yield to the temptation to superficially change his style, but sought doggedly for new elements in his art. This long and laborious process culminated in maturity. A new phase in his life began with the composition of the Fifth Symphony.[1]

The Fifth Symphony at once captured the hearts of its listeners. It was played many times in the winter of 1937 in Moscow, Leningrad and other cities of the Soviet Union. We shall always remember those days—the great concert halls crowded with people, listening delightedly to every chord, every note. A new world opened before the composer then. He had created a symphony of classical perfection. It was a thrilling experience to be present at the "un-

[1] In 1935–1936 Shostakovich worked on the score of his Fourth Symphony. This work was finished and submitted for performance at a concert of the Leningrad Philharmonic Orchestra. After one of the rehearsals, however, the composer withdrew the score and it was never played before the public. A long time has passed, but the composer still keeps the symphony in his portfolio, unwilling to acquaint his audience with this work. There is no need to question his reasons. Suffice it to say that those who are familiar with the score have expressed no doubts as to its value and very much desire to hear it played by an orchestra.

veiling" of that monumental symphony and a great pleasure to know the composer was our countryman. An ovation greeted his appearance on the stage. A high gale of applause expressed the appreciation of the audience.

The content of the Fifth Symphony—"determination of self"—was actually autobiographical in nature: Shostakovich had travelled a long, hard road and was now telling of his tribulations. If the content had been limited to this, however, the symphony would have been interesting merely from a subjective-psychological point of view. Actually, it was far deeper. Shostakovich's story was similar to that of many, and a truthful musical reflection of his experiences could not help but move the hearts of the masses who had come to hear him.

Shostakovich approached his subject very earnestly, found the necessary means to mirror the great pattern of human suffering. To this the symphony owes its vast range of moods: its meditative character and melancholy, its humor and stimulating vitality. It was for this, too, that it resounded throughout the world, that music critics everywhere expressed the opinion that it was indeed a splendid work of contemporary art.

Just as Shakespeare's great tragedy of Macbeth at the very outset foreshadows events to come, the first four bars of the Fifth determine its subsequent course. Those first four bars are indeed an epigraph, live and dramatic, the motive force of the symphony's development.

The theme of the epigraph is ascetically austere. The music is of a restrained, questioning character. The broad initial current tapers to condensed and compact phrases which remind one of an unreleased spring, deceptively still, but harboring the pressure initially applied. . . . This

60

magazine of energy releases a world of musical imagery in the symphony.

The initial theme recedes and only the by now familiar rhythm of the basses reminds one of its latent energy. Upon this "carrier" there rises a listless melody, falling only to rise and fall again—an unmistakable expression of futility and frustration.

There is nothing more terrible than apathy toward life and the forces of the spirit. This must be opposed determinedly, implacably. The strength to overcome inertness and apathy must be found in oneself. Such is the idea of this juxtaposition of two melodies.

The subsequent evolutions of the main theme sketch various phases in the struggle to win free from tormenting reflexes. The symphony unfolds in two directions. There is the mood of reflection and there is the new-born principle of determination, willful and ever stronger. The culminating point draws near. How tense is the melodic ascent of the trombones and French horns! It would seem that the breaking point must be imminent! But here the epigraph is sounded again. New and persistent questions arise and the cycle is closed. There has been no solution. Despite the intensity of polyphonic development and emotional tension there is a return to the symphony's point of departure and therefore to its prior, underlying theme, which now contributes something new—serenity and sonorous melody.

Original too is the harmonic aspect of the underlying subject with its constant modulations and fluid melodic current. This is achieved by Shostakovich's characteristic tone progressions. Varying harmony intensified by the variety of tone color lends this passage particular charm. Violins in the high register are sounded against the serene chords of deeper strings and harps. (Something similar may be found in the first part of the Quintet.) As for the content of the theme, it is lyric and meditative, tinged with sadness and elegiac. One may liken it to the sensation attending reminiscence (memories of the distant past) and reflection (over the remote, inaccessible future).

The staid introductory theme is stirred by another, more vital and dynamic theme. The latter, however, is not yet fated to gain supremacy. Its flow tapers to a cryptic B-flat minor chord carried by clarinet, bassoon and double bassoon.

The Fifth Symphony is indeed varied in emotional content. Here one may find the troubled and questioning modulations, dramatic surges, a stream of elegiac reflections and sombre meditation. Here there is a conglomeration, a labyrinth of feelings! The introductory theme prevailing throughout lends balance and direction to the whole and carries it into a sphere of its own. The beginning of the development is of an ominous character. There is the sternness of thunder in the enunciation of the main theme. Intonations of the epigraph too thrust themselves upon the ear and the subsidiary theme is distorted into an outburst of wild and passionate energy.

At the end of the development the main theme comes in again but altered beyond recognition. Shostakovich reverts to tragic grotesquerie recalling the transformation of the Scherzo of Tchaikovsky's Sixth Symphony and the nightmare metamorphosis of the reverie theme in Scriabin's Ninth Sonata. Here too the musical imagery is suddenly and unexpectedly changed. It is a change of mind expressed in terms of genre (an earnest theme, the concentration of all seriousness is transformed into something very much like a march grotesque) and in terms of timbre. There is something incongruous about the transformation of the main theme which brings to mind a monstrous mask, the frozen grimace of a barbarian menacing mankind. The dramatic impetuosity of this episode carries us far away from the main theme and from the exposition as a whole.

The *recapitulation* is not formally co-ordinated with the exposition though the two are linked by the subject matter. It differs from the general exposition in that the theme of the epigraph predominates while the main theme loses importance. One may say that the full meaning of the epigraph theme is disclosed in the *recapitulation*. As distinct from its condensed and compact introduction it here tends to extend and evolve by rising sequences. This powerful build-up to a climax is somewhat reminiscent of Tchaikovsky's symphonic manner. The *agitato* effect is also heightened by change of tempo. Formerly a lofty and austere Largo, it has now become a swift Allegro.

The second theme of the *recapitulation* may be interpreted as a meditative gaze into the future. The unanswerable introductory questionings, the vain probings and insoluble contradictions evoke a vision of the ideal by force of contrast. The thought of its remoteness and perhaps inaccessibility give rise to an elegiac Coda. The epilogue slowly gains momentum. Against the precise rhythm of the basses (reminiscent of the exposition) the main theme is once more transformed and at last leads to a dramatic cadential section. The epigraph is sounded again by the lower instruments. There is the steady pulsation of the strings and a single violin sings above all. Dull thuds of the kettledrum, descending minor thirds crested by a rising chromatic scale of celesta. . . . It would be difficult to imagine a more perfect and impressive expression of hopelessness and despair.

The first movement of the symphony is exceptionally forceful. The emotional tension increases steadily towards the inevitable—a wild clash of contradictory moods. The exposition with its tormenting mental conflict and lyric reminiscence, with its surges of resolution and intervals of weary submission is repeated in stormy, violent fashion. This leads to the dramatic culmination (beginning of the recapitulation) and thence to the sorrowful awareness of the coda—a world of lost illusions.

The directness of its message, its sincerity and eloquence, its organic unity of form set this music apart from the numerous symphonic scores of modern times. And above all the first movement—an orchestral drama immaculate in form and rich in content which rises to heights of tragic grandeur.

The second movement is a brilliant Scherzo, once more revealing the composer's inexhaustible inventiveness. Differing from many of his previous compositions in its emotional spontaneity and lack of affectation, it symphonizes the waltz or Laendler (somewhat in the tradition of Schubert—or to be more exact—it is a tangent of the Schubert dance, symphonized rather after the style of Mahler).

Here Shostakovich captures the real spirit of the Scherzo —moods clear as crystal and optimism unbounded. It gives us the whole gamut—the flash of wit; the uproarious laughter; the rough and the refined salt of humor.

The first melodic idea is all rhythm—as clear and precise as any dance could be. The subtle humor of the melody with its unexpected turns of harmony, the angular intervals, deliberate brakes on the movement, create its particular originality. This skein of the Scherzo is constantly reiterated and at times suggestions of it appear in other passages. The second subject too is in a dance idiom but its rhythm is much more forceful. The third has an irresistible impact of vitality and radiance.

The fourth melodic idea may be said to be one of the masterpieces of the composer's Scherzo style, combining originality with economy, orchestrated with refinement and transparence of color. It owes its originality to an ingenious treatment of common patterns. The grotesque is here introduced with subtlety and grace. There is something of Mozart in the lightness of this charming melody.

There is many a brilliant stroke in the orchestration of the Scherzo. It is interesting to note that many of the orchestral devices have classical connotations. The entry in unison of the violoncellos and string basses, for example, is analogous to the opening of the Scherzo in Beethoven's Fifth Symphony. The humorous stammering of the bassoons may be found in many works of Beethoven, Mozart and Haydn. The solo trumpets once more remind us of Beethoven's Fifth Symphony. This shows how the composer has shouldered the cloak of the classical traditions, though he wears it in his own original way. Characteristic of Shostakovich is his free dealing with the registers of his instruments, his appreciation of the sonority of chamber music and the fact that he is not afraid of leaving spaces unfilled between orchestral voices.

The dramatic function of the Scherzo is obvious enough. It clears the painfully overcharged atmosphere of the first movement, gives us a concentrated breath of optimism, spiritual health as opposed to spasmodic reflexes. It is an ideal, however, which rises before the composer only for a moment and by vanishing serves to aggravate those troubled thoughts pervading the first movement at the close. From this, too, the third movement of the symphony derives its tragic expression of futility.

This movement attracted the attention of nearly all critics. The reason is obvious. Here they found a world of poetic charm, melodic beauty and warmth of emotion which so moved the hearers. With all due respect to the fine poesy of the Largo, one should, nonetheless, not attribute main importance to this phase of the symphony. Emotionally and dramatically it is poorer than the first movement which actually contains the complete philosophical idea of the symphony. The Largo serves to develop and deepen certain ideas of the first movement. Like the Scherzo it too is monolithic in content and in this differs from the multiphase first movement.

The Largo is a splendid example of Shostakovich's mature style which appears in many pages of his Sixth Symphony and Pianoforte Quintet. It indeed represents a concentration of deep and lyric human emotion. Its spiritual content shows that the composer has won completely free of his formalistic errors of the past.

The Largo is an expression of utter submission to fate. Its lyric warmth is tempered by a certain austerity of color and outline. There is the tragedy and pathos of a will held captive. The stately development of the movement, without a hint of melodramatic *stretto* or *accelerando*, serves to heighten the culminating effect. Something new here in the evolution of the symphony is the fact that a single musical idea begins to predominate. Having passed the troubled searchings of the first movement and paused for an instant

66

with the life-asserting Scherzo, the composer returns to the Largo's sorrowful mood of frustration. This could have served as the tragic epilogue, but such was not the composer's purpose.

The first theme of the Largo is sternly reiterated by the basses. The following pages find Shostakovich at his best. Every line here has its own meaning. There is the soaring melody of the first violins. Though ranging over three octaves, it fades to form a background for the earnest melody of an oboe. Subjective and plaintive, this melodious recitative of the oboe possesses the eloquence of Bach, though differing from the old master in its modern style. It is twice repeated and the final bars of the passage are written in subtle pastel shades. There are the soft voices of two flutes, a rustling tremolo of the violins, a *pizzicato* of the violoncellos, two clear-cut chimes, a superb piece of transparent orchestration.

The *recapitulation* presents the images of the exposition in a new and dramatic light. Submissiveness here changes to a plea, a cry for help. The rustle of the violins is superseded by an ominous muttering of clarinets while the plaint of the flutes gives way to an agitated, tense melody carried by the high register of the violoncellos. The sorrowful images of the exposition attain a tragic character disclosing the depth and force of feeling which had been veiled by that seeming submissiveness. The probing nature of the first movement once more comes to the fore. This emotional increment, however, leads to a fresh decline in the tension, and to sad resignation in the concluding bars.

As the movement draws to a close there is a reiteration of the main musical ideas of the Largo, one by one. The music seems to be melting away, to be fading to stillness.

. . . Precipitated upon this sombre mood of concentration there is the mad rush of the Finale.

The main theme of the Finale bursts forth with the thunder of kettledrums. Masterfully, it alters the stream of musical ideas and lends the last movement a commanding and proud character.

The second theme of the Finale is not so swift, but it is charged with energy and evokes a vast range of emotions. Relieving the tension of the Finale, it touches upon the slow lyric passages of the former movements.

Particularly interesting, with regard to this, are the concluding passages of the symphony. These serve at once to clarify and emphasize the sombre emotion of the Finale's main current. The broad melodies evoked here are somewhat related to the melodic expression of Tchaikovsky.

The recapitulation is once again launched by the kettledrums, though pianissimo now. The rapid pulsation of the growing melodic flow quickly gains a charge of fresh energy, which is released in the bright flourishes of the ending. This increment is built up from constant repetition of the A in the high registers of strings and woodwinds, and on the powerful strains of the main theme of the Finale, a major theme carried by French horns and trombones. Beethoven's symphonies generally end on repetitions of the tonic and dominant. But the tonic chords predominating here round out the symphony and lend it a certain firmness, levelling that instability observable in former movements.

It has often been said and written that the Finale of the Fifth Symphony is something in the nature of a "deus ex machina" and lacks the organic unity characteristic of Tchaikovsky and Beethoven. This is true and untrue. A careful study of the symphony will reveal that no other resolution was possible from that collision of moods which prevails throughout.

The Finale of the Fifth Symphony reveals that at this stage the composer had not as yet completely found himself. He had traversed a long road by the time of its composition, but in the language of philosophy, he had not yet reached that phase of development where internal contradictions must lead to an exchange of old values for new. Quite naturally the music of the symphony could not reach these new values since the composer was not as yet completely conscious of them. Only three years later was the problem of the Finale solved in the concluding movement of the Pianoforte Quintet.

Shostakovich's Fifth Symphony was the fruit which grew from the seeds that were sown in his First Symphony. It was the natural outcome of the complex evolution of his style. At the same time, one may say that it resulted too from the composer's assimilation and transformation of many tendencies in the world of symphonic music. This was noted more than once. Nearly all critics who wrote about it stressed the importance of such influences as those of Mahler, the modern linearists (particularly of Hindemith) and Stravinsky ("Symphony of Psalms"). To this one must add the pronounced influence of the Russian symphonic school. It is noteworthy that foreign critics have often pointed to the connection between the Fifth Symphony and the traditions of the Russian classics. The music critic of the Boston *Christian Science Monitor*, for example, wrote that Shostakovich's music sounded Slavic to a greater degree than any music heard before; that he could take his rightful place beside Mussorgsky, Tchaikovsky and Borodin. Emotion, he continues, is very tense in the score and particularly in the first and third movements. In the slow (third) movement as in the first, the composer seemed particularly to feel those national and racial ties linking him with his musical predecessors. The Scherzo impressed the critic as an expression of national festivity and rejoicing, somewhat crude in its humor, but captivating in its rhythm. He found the Finale the least impressive because of a certain primitiveness, although the structure was sound and the stormy development of its themes recalled the traditions of Tchaikovsky.

This review is particularly interesting for the fact that it mentions Tchaikovsky twice. It is perfectly true that the Fifth Symphony is closely allied to the traditions of the great Russian classicist; his influence upon the composer was no doubt far greater than that of Mahler. Tchaikovsky's influence upon Shostakovich has been previously mentioned. Other examples of a general and detailed character may be set forth.

Allied to the traditions of the Tchaikovsky symphony is the very theme of the Fifth Symphony—the struggle of the human consciousness striving to surmount all obstacles in the path of its distant ideal. The ideals of Tchaikovsky and Shostakovich are different, but there is an affinity between their strivings. Man and his fate hold the principal attention both of Tchaikovsky (in his numerous symphonies) and Shostakovich (in his Fifth Symphony). Their similar problems led to a certain similarity in dramatic principles: an analogy may be drawn between the epigraph of the Fifth Symphony and the famous introduction of Tchaikovsky's F-minor Symphony.

It goes without saying that Tchaikovsky's promptings stimulated Shostakovich, but did not induce him to accept this influence in an academic-epigonic manner. Realization of this will facilitate a proper understanding of one of the finest symphonic works of our times.

Those who had followed the development of Shostakovich's talent discerned fresh horizons in his Fifth Symphony. Its lyricism, passion, emotions tender and pure, sad and joyous, its variety of ideas could not help but move all who acquainted themselves with this symphonic masterpiece. Whereas Shostakovich's art formerly bore traces of affectation, this music was a sincere and truthful story of his life-experience.

One more thing should be mentioned. In Shostakovich's Fifth Symphony for the first time we find the element of the moral and esthetic. The talent of the composer had obviously grown and matured. He had approached the most serious and intricate artistic problems of his times. He had approached them armed with great skill and originality of style. His contemporaries will find it difficult properly to evaluate the merits and demerits of his work. Their certainty of the classic perfection of his Fifth Symphony, however, is undoubtedly justified.

In 1937, the year he finished his Fifth Symphony, Shostakovich became a professor of the Leningrad Conservatory. At first he taught instrumentation, but later directed a class in composition. He did not believe that teaching was his proper calling, but contrary to his own expectations, he became a brilliant teacher and instructor of gifted Soviet youth. Within a short time his class yielded a series of young and very promising composers. Shostakovich the artist has exercised much charm not only on his pupils, but on the wider circles of young musicians. Distinguished for his breadth of vision, he is not inclined to orientate his pupils upon his own achievements. From his student composers he demands a thorough knowledge of the musical literature of the world. The better to facilitate the development of each, he strives to acquaint them with all that is important.

CHAPTER V

LYRIC INTERMEZZO

THE FURTHER COURSE of the composer was clearly defined. Other works equally important in content and mature in conception could be expected from him. These expectations were justified by his Pianoforte Quintet. He reverted to the theme of his Fifth Symphony when he found a fresh expression for it in his Seventh Symphony dedicated to the valor of the Soviet people in defense of their country. Before he wrote these scores, however, he had written two others developing certain ideas of the Fifth Symphony in a somewhat less complex and profound manner. This refers to his String Quartet and Sixth Symphony.

It was only natural that the stormier flight of his imagination should be followed by a period of tranquillity. The most tense and turbulent works of the great composers were often followed by calmer compositions. Shostakovich's Fifth was similarly followed by the String Quartet, a lyric intermezzo born of his free flight of fantasy in a moment of creative relaxation after the completion of a great and difficult work.

The String Quartet seems a modest sort of composition as compared with the grandeur of the Fifth Symphony, but it too is indicative of the new phase in the composer's development. It attests to his creative range and versatility in

73

dealing with the most varied artistic ideas. Simple and melodic, the score contains no redundant frills and recalls the finest pages of Schubert's romantic music. There are no wild moments here (except for a passage in its remarkable Scherzo). The composition reminds one of a quiet rivulet wending its way through forests and fields. Its straightforwardness and poetic naiveté lend it especial charm. No bright contrasts may be found in a single one of its four movements. It is light, airy, reserved and very expressive.

There are no sombre hues in the lucid and harmonious Moderato of the first movement. It is bright and naive, serene and graceful. Though reflective, it is never passive, but pervaded with dance rhythms, the unhurried movement of the slow minuet or saraband.

The very first theme is full of poetic charm. Characteristic are its simplicity, smooth continuity of melody, even rhythm and lucid harmony (barring individual angularities). It derives much of its color from resounding consecutive sixths. The first theme is in the nature of a dialogue between the first violin and the violoncello. This is accompanied by continuous thirds carried by the violas and second violins.

The second theme is equally light and calm. The melody paces firmly over the swelling tone of the violin. It is accompanied by *glissando* passages of the violoncello and the reiteration of a single note by the viola. Here too the principle of the dialogue prevails.

Unforgettable is the coda. The harmonic beauty and vivid emotion of the first movement is here concentrated in several bars. This is one of those rare musical finds which at once seizes upon the memory, pursues the listener, charms and inspires him.

There is a fine radiant effect in the flow of thirds in the

final measures when the themes of the first movement fade to wisps of melody.

The second movement—Moderato—proceeds in the same calm gait. Also of a reflective nature, it is tinged with melancholy. However there is nothing sombre about this melancholy. It is but a light, lyric sadness, essentially untroubled. Somewhat contrasting the brighter first movement, it is at the same time closely allied to it. It is actually a tangent of the same mood.

The broad and sonorous Moderato, practically for the first time in Shostakovich's chamber music, reveals something of national color. The plagal cadences and vast melodic current ally it to the broad melodies of old Russia and recall the atmosphere of the Volga steppes.

The Moderato is a theme with variations. The sonorous melody is scarcely changed in all the variations. Only the timbres, registers and textures are changed.

The composer deliberately limited himself to these modest means of expression. He wished to present his theme in various colors and thereby impress its beauty upon the listener. Simple though his principles were, he managed to achieve a remarkable effect. His variations are very finely woven, diverse in color and of great lyric and melodic beauty. As for the theme, it may be said to be one of the finest inspirations of the composer.

There is something elusive in the flight of the Scherzo (allegro molto). Carried by muted strings it passes swiftly and softly. The pattern here is woven of the finest polyphonic webs. This music may be likened to a whimsical interplay of shadows or the shifting patterns of clouds by night. There is something phantasmal and mysterious about the tonality.

The Scherzo is subdivided into three parts. There is a

restless movement to the rhythm in the first and third parts. There are many delicate points here. Surprising is the composer's ability to attain a fresh tone-color with two or three strokes. This was done with grace and lightness in his previous Scherzos. Later he created yet another of his polished Scherzos in the second movement of the Sixth Symphony.

The Finale, the largest movement, is cheerful and sunny as a summer morning. The twilight hues of the Scherzo have faded. There are no emotional contrasts here. Both themes of the Finale express the same feeling of well being. The music is permeated with true Mozartian vitality, subsequently reiterated by the composer in the two last movements of his Sixth Symphony as well as in the Finale of his Pianoforte Quintet. The "Mozartian" quality in the music of Shostakovich is not due to any stylistic imitation of the classic composer of "Don Juan," but rather to its being similar in clarity, harmoniousness and melodic action.

There is something mischievous and mirthful in the main theme of the Finale: Its light, fluttering rhythms and soft melodies culminate in resounding chords. The second theme is calm and even. Swift and buoyant, the development of the two furnishes rhythmic and dynamic contrast.

Important in the development of the Finale is its uninterrupted movement: The music flows lightly and unconstrained, charmingly odd in its sudden contrasts, subtle humor and cheerfulness. The slow lyric passages of the Quartet are here repeated in lively dance form, a play of joyous feeling.

Far from being complex in content, Shostakovich's Quartet is even naive. All the more striking is its beauty of

76

harmony. The music discloses the composer's new world of sentiment, it reflects awareness of his creative potential, lyrical elation expressive of the new phase in his development and that of Soviet music as a whole. Reflection of a new and beautiful ideal—such is the meaning of Shostakovich's Quartet.

Soviet theorists have only just turned their attention to the problems of the new esthetics. The nihilistic negation of esthetic values is a thing of the past. How curious the old assertion would sound today that the very conception of beauty in art was obsolete and that it must be consigned to the scrap heap of history. The development of Soviet art shows that the opposite is true: More and more often do works of art appear which unmistakably strive for the ideal of beauty. In music this is true of Shostakovich's Quartet, the 21st Symphony of Myaskovsky, the "Poem to Stalin" and the Violin Concerto of Khachaturyan.

At present it is difficult fully to appraise the esthetic ideal as expressed in the scores of Shostakovich, Myaskovsky and Khachaturyan. I should like only to point out that the esthetic element in the best productions of modern art is not something created in a vacuum. Its inspiration comes not from retirement into realms of abstract reflection, but from contact with the very heart of life.

Now a few remarks on the specific features of the expression of the esthetic ideal as found in Shostakovich's Quartet. Characteristic is its brevity of form and laconic manner of execution, its restraint, the composer's sense of balance and ability to get the most out of the simplest means of expression. In this the Quartet differs from the Violin Concerto of Khachaturyan where the ideal of beauty is unfolded most generously, with tempestuous

77

emotion, flourishing colors and violent rhythms. Should one compare these works with those of the great painters, one might say that the Quartet is somewhat akin to the esthetics of Raphael and the Concerto, to the esthetics of Rubens. Both, needless to say, are of equal value. The esthetic ideal may be variously expressed. Shostakovich's Quartet was merely one means of its expression.

No sooner had he finished the Fifth Symphony than Shostakovich began to work on another large composition. He had decided to write a vocal symphonic composition dedicated to Vladimir Ilyich Lenin. Aware of the responsibility of his task, he labored long and hard. "To embody in art the gigantic figure of this leader is going to be an incredibly difficult task," he wrote in one of his articles. "I am well aware of this and when I speak of the content of my symphony I am, of course, not thinking of historical events, of biographical facts connected with Vladimir Ilyich, but only of the general theme, the general idea of this work. I have pondered long over the means of dealing with this theme in music. I have conceived of my symphony as a work for orchestra, chorus and soloists. I have made a careful study of the poetry and literature devoted to Vladimir Ilyich and will have to write a vocal score for the symphony. The text will consist mainly of Mayakovsky's verses about Lenin. In addition, I intend to use the best of the folk tales and folk songs about Ilyich and the verses that were written about him by the poets of the fraternal republics. I am not afraid to introduce the works of various poets about Lenin. The text will owe its wholeness and continuity mainly to those sentiments which are evoked by every word of the people about Lenin. That wholeness too must be preserved by the symphony which must be unified throughout in content and means of expression. The symphony will not only draw upon the words of the folk songs about Lenin, but also upon their melodies." [1]

Realizing the need to gather more material, the composer for a time abandoned his idea and wrote the score which is now known as his Sixth Symphony. Then he returned to his symphonic narrative of Lenin. The newspapers periodically reported on his progress. Once again, however, his plans were not destined to be realized. The Second World War began and in besieged Leningrad Shostakovich wrote a magnificent symphony dedicated to the valor and heroism of the Soviet people.

The Sixth Symphony evoked lively criticism and discussion. Its evaluation was by no means as unanimous as in the case of the Fifth Symphony. He had been expected to write a symphony as full of action, development and dramatic unity as his Fifth. But he "thwarted" his public by producing a work which, though highly finished, was cast in entirely different artistic terms. This was a disappointment to many, and prevented them from perceiving the esthetic value, and understanding the true content, of the symphony.

The Sixth Symphony is largely a negation, and, at the same time, a continuation, of the tendencies evidenced by the Fifth. Its first movement evolves a train of musical thought akin to the sorrowful Largo of its predecessor, but expresses it differently: This music is more reserved and removed from direct emotion. The Scherzo of the Fifth Symphony is related to the second and third movements of the Sixth, which likewise express great elation. The last two

[1] Dmitri Shostakovich: "My Work on the Lenin Symphony," *Literary Newspaper*, Sept. 20, 1938.

movements are a negation of the first. This, in the main, is the constructive principle of the Sixth Symphony.

It was precisely this principle which proved a stumbling block to many in their appraisal of Shostakovich's works. The lack of legitimate hinges between the movements aroused indignation. No one denied the composer's right to pose subjects of various content against one another. But this was at variance with the customary conception of the symphonic cycle, of the thematic and dramatic interrelation of its individual movements. As a matter of fact, the Sixth Symphony owes its force precisely to the vivid contrast of two main subjects, expressions of two varying psychological conditions. The complete resignation and introspection of the Largo serves to emphasize the vitality of the two Scherzos, reminiscent of the sparkling symphonic and operatic finales of Haydn, Mozart and Rossini. The idea of the Sixth Symphony may be allegorically explained as a juxtaposition of the past and the present. The past, belonging to a world of tormenting struggle for the liberation of the human spirit, is retrospectively expressed in the first movement and accounts for the restrained and introspective character of the music. The present is sheer exaltation in victory, ecstasy, and lends the music its airy, carefree character. The artistic principles have grown simpler. The composer has renounced what was redundant and has limited himself to the essential. Laconic expression and wise thrift are characteristic of the style of this symphony and in this respect it was indeed superior to anything written by the composer up to that time.

The first movement of the symphony, the Largo, is something in the nature of a sombre monologue. There are certain features here common to the Largo of the Fifth

Symphony, but the narrative is graver, the resignation greater and the statement more objective. That which expressed past suffering in the Fifth became an objective narrative of the distant past in the Sixth Symphony. Like the fugue of the Quintet, the first movement of the Sixth is merely a reminiscence of tragedy experienced in the past.

The principal constructive features of the Largo are its continuous melodic line, fluidity and changeability. Dramatic conflict of emotion of the classical symphony is lacking here. Instead there is the dynamic linear development reverting to the pre-classical principles akin to the art of Bach. Unfolding the steady movement of a single melody Shostakovich here reminds one of the mighty introductory chorus of the "Passion According to St. Matthew." [2]

Somewhat austere, the main theme of the Largo recalls some melodic patterns of Bach, the progression from the sixth down to the leading note recalls the theme of the G-minor fugue in the first part of the Well-Tempered Clavichord, or the A-minor fugue of the second. The general clarity and simplicity of expression is not lessened by certain harmonic angularities. It is to the clash of plain chords and from complex harmonies that the music owes its singularity.

The meditative nature of the Largo is already apparent in its broad main theme. There is the whisper of minor thirds from the basses; imperceptibly they assume a scale-like movement. It is against this background that the violins sound their sonorous melody which rises constantly to higher registers, alters its timbre, but retains its tranquil,

[2] No comparison is here attempted of the scale and historic significance of these works, but merely of their common principles of melodic development.

81

resigned and melancholy character. A certain tension is then introduced; fragments of sharp sounds cut in upon the harmonic evenness. At the end, however, only the soft trill of the violas remains.

The middle part of the Largo resolves itself into several passages equally calm and restrained, but more varied in melody. The recitative, declamatory element comes more clearly to the fore, the meditation of the first pages is deepened, the music grows slower. Continuous trills lend color to the whole.

The Largo concludes with the mood of tragic resignation. In character and content its resolution approximates the coda of the first movement in the Fifth Symphony. The sad resignation of the coda, however, is the result of an unsolved conflict of emotions. A plaint of the uncertainty of the past, it expresses a moment of great weariness and thereby alleviates the tension of the dramatic collision. The coda here merely expresses the essence of what has passed and sets forth the content of the Largo as separated from definite manifestations. Thought here dominates over emotion. Shostakovich achieves a concentration of thought through aphoristic treatment of his thematic material.

It is impossible to discuss all the merits in the orchestration of the Largo. For this it would be necessary to analyse the score bar by bar. One may merely mention individual and most impressive passages. Such are the introductory bars—a severe unison of cor Anglais, clarinets, bassoons, violas and violoncellos. Such too is the rendition of the main theme by the violins against the even pace of violoncellos and double basses. The composer here made the most of quintet timbres. The low registers alternate with the tense registers of the violins and high violoncellos. A remarkable effect is obtained by descending chromatic trills (piccolo, flute, soprano clarinet, violins and doubled an octave lower by the oboes, clarinets in Bb, cor Anglais, violas and violoncellos). Singular is the recitative of the flute accompanied by soft trills of the violas and violoncellos. These passages are noteworthy for their fine precision to the smallest detail. The same is true of the remaining two movements of the symphony.

The coda comes as the conclusion of a long train of musical thought, an admission of futility. And yet, it only seems to tell a tale of that which has passed, that which is no more, and this, perhaps, is why the sense of disappointment is so easily effaced by the subsequent movements. In this negation there is also a dialectical instant of integrity. The Sixth Symphony therefore does not consist of three separated themes, but is a single musical entity with unified content and a continuous idea throughout.

It is this inter-relation of ideas upon which the separate movements of the symphony are hinged. Their affinity is of an esthetic and not of a technical nature and is therefore less readily perceived through customary analysis of rhythm, melody and harmony than in other compositions of Shostakovich.

The second and third movements transport the listener to a world of subtle nuances and intoxicating exultation. All is brilliant here and the flight of fantasy recalls the sparkling finales of Mozart and Haydn. The Sixth Symphony was born of a live creative impulse in the mind of the composer under the influence of modern Soviet times and events. Despite the partial affinity of its thematic intonation and emotional character with the older works, the music of the Sixth is singular in its assimilation of the classical traditions.

The second movement, an Allegro, is a fairy-like Scherzo and one of the best ever written by Shostakovich. The composer here abandons himself to his favorite swift orchestral paradoxes. This penchant first appeared in the Scherzo of the First Symphony and later unfolded in many of his orchestra passages. At times he indulged in it for its own sake and then it was meaningless, since true art was superseded by brilliant superficial effects. In the Scherzo of the Sixth, Shostakovich showed that he had preserved his ability to achieve the most astonishing orchestral effects, but here they served to express his moods gracefully and whimsically. His technique moreover had grown finer since he had rid himself of that which was redundant. Here, all is in good taste and pleasing by its vividness, variety of color, rhythm and brilliance.

The Scherzo abounds in contrasts of subjects, timbres and rhythms. Though varied, the themes are well knit by related rhythms. Owing to their unity of genre the contrasting subjects merge to form a single musical entity which is at the same time rich in odd melodic diversity.

The first theme of the Scherzo passes like a breath of air in the graceful gait of a minuet or waltz. As is usual in Shostakovich's music, it encompasses a considerable range of registers high and low. The development of the subject is broad. Its main melody varies as it gathers polyphonic undercurrents. Its crisp beat, however, does not change. The second theme is more restrained, but more definitely approximates the waltz, or rather the old "Laendler" with its characteristic triple time rhythm. Its character reminds one of many passages from the classic symphonies. Simple though it seems, however, it is rendered complicated by a polytonal harmonic background.

Finally, there is the third theme in the nature of a broad dialogue between the lower voices of violoncellos and double basses and the higher voices of violins. Pace and motion distinguish it from the preceding dance-like themes.

Characteristic of the Scherzo are its odd and unexpected auxiliary thematic web, new subsidiary melodies. This adds interest to the composer's methods of linking diverse elements. Splendid too is the ease of his polyphonic style. How unconstrained and smoothly the themes fall in with the subvoices, how lucid the texture of the Scherzo! A two voice setting prevails nearly throughout, but the composer made most skilful use of this limitation. Adherence to the linear principle is particularly important where only two voices are to be dealt with and it is this polyphonic construction of the Scherzo that secures independence for each of the two melodic lines.

The brilliant Finale, we believe, is the best part of the symphony. There is complete harmony of form and content here. Its language is simple. The means of expression are those to which listeners have been accustomed from the times of the great Viennese classics, and yet the music is of today. The Finale cannot help but charm the listener by its richness of melody, brilliance of orchestration and particularly by its youthful vitality. This music may indeed be interpreted as creative consciousness at play and utterly free of prejudice and tortuous erring. "The world is wonderful," the composer seems to say, and this admission answers the self-searching questionings of the Fifth Symphony. Like the String Quartet, the Finale of the Sixth Symphony attests to victory over the reflexes, to the attainment of a clear world outlook. In this sense, the Finale of the Sixth is more profound than that of the Fifth, since new qualities here have completely resolved the contradictions of the past. It too, however, is not the synthetic outcome of the symphony's development and is sufficiently linked with its initial and introductory phase. This problem was fully solved for the first time in the Pianoforte Quintet where the Finale organically evolved from the preceding movements as the only possible conclusion of the composition's development and at the same time displayed a fresh quality denying that which had preceded it and signifying a transition to a new psychological condition.

By the nature of its rhythm the main theme of the Finale recalls the gallop. Shostakovich, one may remember, resorted to the gallop in many of his early compositions. In most cases then it bore the nature of parody. But here this genre has been cleared of the superficial and the vulgar. It has become natural and human, and therefore particularly effective. Shostakovich, moreover, invested this theme with fresh meaning and emphasized its flitting and playful character. The lightness of touch here reminds one of a fine etching.

Equally playful and graceful is the second theme. Even more carefree, the gracenotes of the woodwinds emphasize its light humor. Its technique, though modest, is evolved with consummate skill.

The middle part begins with a weighty motion of the basses. Pitted against this in the highest register there is an unconstrained melody which by its burly cheerfulness recalls the Scherzo of the Pianoforte Quintet. In the last pages of the Finale's middle passage the composer merges his whimsical and roguish rhythms. Though difficult to play, it is not likely to strike the hearer as something complicated. There is nothing unnatural about its intermittent beat.[3]

The Fifth Symphony depicts ascension over tormenting doubts and reflects a period of "self-searching." The Sixth draws principal attention to that high spirit which has been attained in arduous and dogged struggle and this symphony therefore may be regarded as something in the nature of an "epilogue" to its predecessor. Subsequently, Shostakovich proved able to combine the contradicting elements of his Fifth and Sixth Symphonies in a single composition in his Pianoforte Quintet.

The Sixth Symphony is noteworthy for its highly finished style. The composer's fresh outlook finds expression in harmonious and classical forms and this signifies his victory over disharmony and confusion. The Fifth and Sixth Symphonies of Shostakovich, like his later chamber music, are complete and well-rounded expressions of definite cycles of ideas and emotions. His further development required new themes and fresh artistic imagery.

Today it is clear that the Sixth Symphony was a logical phase in the development of the composer's gifts (and not a deviation as some critics believed), that it was a work characteristic of a definite phase of Soviet music (and did not stray from the tendencies of the latter as the very same critics claimed). Perfectly clear too is the lack of comprehension of the symphony displayed by listeners and critics alike. (The symphony has never been properly appraised since both those who severely criticized the content and style and the rash eulogizers who could not seem to lavish

[3] The rhythm in this passage owes its complexity to linear development and not to those semi-rhythmic complications which result from juxtapositions in themselves of simple rhythms of various voices, a method far more frequently applied by composers.

sufficient praise on this work, could not penetrate to the essence of its music).

Today we attribute to the Sixth Symphony a special place between the composer's dramatic narrative of personal tragedy and his heroic symphonic poem wherein individuality is invisibly bound with the social whole. The Sixth Symphony will continue to exemplify the mature style of the composer. It may, indeed, be termed the progenitor of the Pianoforte Quintet.

CHAPTER VI

TO THE HEIGHTS OF PHILOSOPHICAL LYRICISM

F<small>EW WORKS OF ART</small> met with such instant appreciation as the Pianoforte Quintet of Shostakovich. Its very first renditions brought triumph to the composer.[1] The listeners were truly inspired by the beauty of the music. None could be indifferent. The artistic value of the composition was self-evident. That first impression, moreover, has proved lasting and is justified to the present. One might even say that the significance of the Quintet has been growing from day to day. Its classical perfection is becoming more and more evident. The Quintet is not only one of the best works of the composer, but also an outstanding achievement of modern music as a whole. Just recognition of this was the Stalin Prize, First Class, conferred upon the composer.

The theme of the Quintet is not alien to that of the Fifth Symphony. The composer once more refers to the "determination of self," once more tells of victory over spiritual disharmony, of that clarity of conception achieved

---

[1] The Quintet was first played in the Small Hall of the Conservatory in Moscow, on November 23, 1940, by the composer and the members of the Beethoven Quartet: D. Tsyganov, V. Shirinsky, V. Borisovsky and S. Shirinsky.

in hard struggle. There is a vital difference between the two works, of course. It is not a difference in genre (as some suppose), but in the personal and artistic evolution of the composer. Shostakovich approached his Quintet armed with that clarity of conception which came to him from his String Quartet and the Mozartian brilliance which marked his Sixth Symphony. The Quintet, it will be noted, was written at a time when he had fully overcome his former Hamlet-like reflexes. This accounts for its vividness, clarity and objectivity. Whereas tragic pathos predominated in the Fifth Symphony, this composition was swayed by philosophical lyricism. Former tribulations of the spirit are retrospectively posed by the Fugue which passes to the lyricism of the intermezzo and the ecstatic Finale which rises over the entire work like a graceful arch.

The Pianoforte Quintet was written for the traditional instruments: 2 violins, viola, violoncello and piano. It consists of five movements: Prelude (Lento G-minor), Fugue (Adagio G-minor), Scherzo (Allegretto B-major), Intermezzo (Lento D-minor), and Finale (Moderato poco allegretto G-major).

The first movement is clearly and laconically set forth in three-part form (Lento-Poco più Mosso-Lento). The first of the three, austerely magnificent, contains the thematic germ of the composition. Softly lyrical, the second emerges with ease from the compact first and returns to it with equal naturalness.

The first and second themes are variously executed. The full body of the quintet is used for the one, while individual instruments speak for the other against a clear-cut pianoforte background. Characteristic of the first passage of the Prelude is the organ-like sonority (the pianoforte does not merge with the voices of the quartet, but stands out against them as a separate timbre, somewhat resembling that of the organ).

The introductory passage, a Largo, is somewhat akin to the epigraph theme of the Fifth Symphony. Not imperious like its predecessor, however, it does seem to express a solemn acceptance of vital problems.

The content of the Prelude is by no means exhausted in the first of its subjects. It is further developed in the *Poco più mosso* passage. A graceful and rhythmical minuet replaces the former measured movement, its pattern becomes light and transparent. The melody carried by the viola is replete with charming lyricism. The piano pursues its own line of melody which merges beautifully with the viola's theme. This is followed by the violin which carries the noble melody to the highest register.

The softness of the middle passage lends particular austerity and magnificence to the Largo. As is usual in Shostakovich's music, a dynamic recapitulation follows here; only the tonal web is heavier and the execution more complex. The canonic reiteration of the main theme (by pianoforte and quartet) may serve as a splendid example of the composer's consummate treatment of his material.

The Fugue is closely linked with the Prelude and seems to lend objectivity to the former's lyric content. The two are allied in subject matter—the melodic nucleus of the Fugue was taken from the main theme of the Prelude, as well as the emotional quality, since the emotional content of the Prelude finds its continuation here. The concentrated air of the introduction is transformed to philosophic meditation warmly colored by its lyrical feeling.

This Fugue of Shostakovich is exceptional for its technique and esthetic value. Though earnest to the point of austerity it is divorced from that scholasticism which may be discerned in the fugues of so many composers. Shostakovich is master of his polyphony which in his hands attains the eloquence of language. Even his most complex orchestration is guided less by calculation than by musical principle and the ease with which he copes with all difficulties is phenomenal.

The simple and sonorous melody of the Fugue is in a minor key. Developing unhurriedly, its wistful charm reminds one of the flowing melodies of the Russian folk song. Such an impression would not at all be subjective. Despite its melodic principles, which would seem none too near those of Russian folk melody, it is decidedly related to the latter. Its nostalgia recalls the vastness of Russia's plains and wooded lands—perhaps as painted by the brush of Isaac Levitan.

Quietly, unhurriedly the instruments pick up the subject of the Fugue one by one. It descends step by step until, at the end of the exposition, it is sounded in the bass register of the piano. The entire exposition is restrained and calm, the melodic lines too are unraveled slowly, and the sonority is muted (*con sord* strings and soft bass notes of the piano).

The continuous and rhythmic motion leads to a culminating point, and pervades the theme of the Fugue, though it can be perceived only intermittently. This intermittence is overcome and thereby the theme of the Fugue is altered. The broadening melody grows more intense and finally revives the main theme of the Prelude. First the piano and then the violoncello pick up one of the most vivid and tense melodies of the Prelude, thus introducing an element of pathos and preparing the way for the recapitulation.

Remarkable for the refinement of its polyphony, the recapitulation does not at first disclose the whole subtle pattern woven by the composer. Its very simplicity and naturalness are a tribute to his skill.[2]

The conclusion of the Fugue is charged with emotion. Like a final word of counsel, a rhythmic intonation in the bass repeats the theme of the Fugue and at the same time reiterates the melody of the violoncello and the final cadenzas of the first passage.

The general trend of the Fugue is not governed by abstract ideas. Intensely human, it is a most convincing reflection of life, earnest, warm and spontaneous.

In its verve, temperament and vitality, the Scherzo offers a sharp contrast to the two austere preceding movements. There is something elementary in the sonority of its major thirds and vigorous rhythms, but it is precisely this quality which serves the composer as a most effective means of expression.

In content and dramatic import this movement is similar to the Scherzo of the Fifth Symphony. In both cases the sombre hues of doubt (pathetic in the Fifth Symphony, but philosophical and objective in the Quintet) are dispelled by brighter colors. This is even more true of the Quintet than of the symphony. More laconic, compact and simple, it is

[2] *Stretto* on the theme already occurs in the first bars of the Fugue (first and second violins). Retarded by a fourth, the second violin may be said to present a fresh counter-exposition of the theme. Especially interesting is the fact that when the third voice enters and the theme continues its flow in the stretto of the second violin and viola, this stretto fits harmoniously to the second stretto carried by the first violin and its violoncello companion.

also more convincing. The best of Shostakovich's Scherzos were always remarkable for their ingenuity, pithiness and impulsive rhythms and this is true of the Scherzo in his Quintet which differs from its predecessors, however, by its greater simplicity of expression. Its dancing gait recalls the robust humor of the minuets of Haydn and Beethoven. A torrent of colorful sounds, these passages cling to the memory.

The main theme of the Scherzo is purposeful, determined and well defined throughout. Its energetic pace loosens a variety of scale-like passages. The velocity of the scales is soon checked by the continuous reiteration of F-G-F on the piano. The second theme, a melody delicately traced, differs from the first by its spontaneity and capricious humor. Interesting is the passage wherein the theme is modified in the high chiming register of the piano against the clear-cut rhythmic chords of the strings. This procedure, characteristic of Shostakovich's pianoforte style, also lends unique color to that episode of the Quintet.

The Intermezzo invokes the mood of the first two movements, though in a different manner. That air of severity in the introduction and the rapt concentration of the Fugue give way to poetic lyricism, warmth and spontaneity. The music is touching for the purity and delicacy of its emotion. It is indeed one of the few works of music that at once grips the attention, charms the listener and impresses itself on his memory as a poetic musical image not to be forgotten.

The Intermezzo is governed by the free flow of its melody. It is voiced by the violin, in the duet of the violin and viola, the dialogue of two violins and of the viola and violoncello (the duet of the violins forms a canon with that

94

of the viola and violoncello).[3] Though there are no sharp contrasts in this movement, its principal moods are evolved in many shades. A world of lyrical emotion is opened before the listener here. The soft conclusion of the Intermezzo gives rise to the theme of the Finale.

Bright and unclouded, the Finale, as it were, furnishes the answers to questions previously raised. The composer evidently felt that a Finale of the usual magnificent and triumphant sort would scarcely be justified. The austere philosophical lyricism of the Fugue is dissolved here and the Scherzo is reiterated with fresher spirit, and more joyously. In exceptionally harmonious terms the music of the Finale expresses happiness, serenity and contentment won in the turmoil of life. Presenting a synthesis of the previous movements, the composer here finds the solution for all contradictions which they had posed. The Finale, in other words, solves all problems of the composition, whether of a musical or psychological nature.

The Finale is based on two themes, varied in genre, but tonally related. The first is serene, simple, but very original.[4] The second at first appears in the high register of the piano against the rhythmic strumming of the strings (*pizzicato*). As unassuming as the first in melody, its tempo is something in the nature of a march. Encompassing

[3] The viola is introduced in a most delicate manner. The main melody carried by the violin terminates on the tonic D. This note is then doubled by the viola which joins the violin. Now the viola gradually descends to an interval of a third (D-C-B) while the D is still held by the violin. This way the interval of a third is established between the two instruments for the start of the duet.

[4] How fresh is the effect of the sudden decline by a third in the next to the last measure (to B)! The reiteration of B heightens the color. No less unique is the alternate repetition of the major and diminished seventh.

a generous range, it strides boldly over broad intervals within a span of two octaves.

Most original is the transition to the recapitulation. The intonation of the Prelude, though easily recognized, is slightly modified in the high register of the violin. As if reiterating that which had gone before, at the same time it serves to contrast the Finale and to round out the whole of the composition.

The recapitulation reconstructs the exposition not on a greater, but on a smaller scale. This, however, does not impoverish the content. Though brief, the recapitulation introduces certain elements which were absent in the exposition. The simplicity of intonation and harmonic structure is here and there relieved by unique and subtle innuendoes.[5]

The Finale concludes with a quiet diminuendo passage sustained by fresh G major chords. Bright and serene, it resolves all preceding contradictions.

Shostakovich's Quintet is remarkable for its rich and profound content. This truly inspired score unfolds the world of rich imagination and deep feelings of a gifted artist. Its clearly defined emotion, optimism and integrity are undoubtedly its chief merits.

The constructive principles of the Quintet and its genres (prelude, fugue) are reminiscent of the seventeenth- and eighteenth-century masters. Shostakovich on the whole seems to have by-passed the traditions of the Viennese classicists who established the standards of chamber music which had lost little of its significance for the Romanticists and even for the composers of the beginning of the twen-

---

[5] A unique interval in the final phrase of the piano are the alternating notes of E-flat and E, F-sharp and F.

tieth century. The Quintet, however, is as well knit as the chamber music of Mozart and Beethoven. The principles of the classical and pre-classical epochs are generously and rationally applied. The classical features of the Quintet appear in the construction of its movements which are well proportioned and logically rounded out. Each train of musical thought is evolved to its natural conclusion.

Important for the rendition and interpretation of the composition is the fact that the composer rarely availed himself of full sonority. This enlarges the gamut of the composition and intensifies its culminating passages. He is fond of tracing delicate melodies one against the other, prefers to limit himself to duets and trios carried in turn by various combinations of the five instruments. Noteworthy too is the fact that the composer at times managed to widen the framework of the Quintet and to achieve six timbres. In certain passages the piano presents two separate polyphonic currents on its opposite registers.

As in the case of his Quartet, the composer here too strove for continuous melody and sonority. This pertains firstly to the strings whose sonorous qualities were used to the full. The strict simplicity of style, based on expressive elements rather than virtuosity, is also linked with the traditions of the old masters. The piano score too is governed by the melodic principle. Unison and octave passages are frequent. There is the "hollow" ring of widely separated voices. Shostakovich is fond of simple melodic lines stripped of frills and virtuosity. For this reason, the pianoforte, in most cases functions as a string instrument.

The polyphony of the Quintet should and must become the object of careful study. The most difficult technical problems here are solved with surprising ease. It would seem that the themes by themselves link up with one another to form subtle canons and complex strettos. Shostakovich's polyphony, moreover, is not only justified for its construction, but also for its emotional content. For this reason it is easy to comprehend despite its complexity. One may even say that the complexity of his polyphony helps to clarify the content.

The Pianoforte Quintet followed logically from Shostakovich's development as an artist and was, of course, the best of his chamber music compositions. In connection with this one should mention the general qualities of his chamber music.

Shostakovich displayed thorough understanding of the chamber music ensemble, the ability to make the most of the individual instruments and, at the same time, to merge them all into a single whole. In none of his chamber music composition does he pursue the beaten track, but everywhere breaks boldly with accepted custom, creates his own style while orientating himself on the traditions of the great masters.

Shostakovich has lent new meaning to the various principles of chamber music. Here again he has turned to the traditions of the seventeenth- and eighteenth-century masters, their manner of making fullest use of the concert properties of individual instruments, their choice of genres and certain methods of expression (many details in the Quintet remind one of the style of Bach or Handel). There is not a shade of affectation of the archaic here. Though one may recognize certain traditions of the old masters in Shostakovich's music, he invariably uses them in his own and modern way. He is invariably himself.

In addition to the classic influences in Shostakovich's

chamber music one may discern those of modern composers, particularly of Paul Hindemith. As has been observed, the linear principles played an important role in the development of Shostakovich's art. This was differently manifested at different stages of his development. Whereas the linear principles were formerly uncritically applied (in his string octet), the composer in his later compositions rid himself of all that was redundant and, having gained a good grasp of certain valuable elements, evolved his own musical ideas.

In the best of his chamber pieces Shostakovich strove for simplicity of rendition and clarity of instrumentation. Whereas the chamber music of the Romanticists tended to grow more and more complex in rendition, and that of the Impressionists acquired ever more unusual color effects (unusual in the sense that they were decked with unusual trappings for the sake of odd effects), Shostakovich pursued his own path: Linear effects in his compositions superseded oddness of tonality. This may also be found in the works of the Western linearists, but Shostakovich's graphic effects are more concrete, more alive. Combinations of abstract melodies in his works have given way to the inspired, emotional and charmingly simple melody.

Whereas most classical and romantic works of chamber music begin in allegro tempo, Shostakovich's violoncello sonata, his Quartet and Quintet begin with the more serene Allegretto, Moderato or Lento. Slow tempos, moreover, prevail in the remaining movements of these works. This is particularly true of the Quintet. Not a movement here is written in a fast tempo. The Scherzo proceeds in Allegretto and even the Finale reveals none of the usual acceleration. This is reminiscent of the old masters who were fond of

99

launching their largest works with a slow movement. Allegro and Presto then signified slower tempos than in our days.

The prevalence of slow tempos lends an air of grandeur and serenity to Shostakovich's chamber music and particularly so to his Quintet. At the same time, his compositions do not seem unduly long or drawn-out as so many works of this kind do, owing to lack of tempo contrasts. There is a meaningful progression to Shostakovich's music. Though slow, his movements come alive owing to their rhythmic development. There is still action behind the unhurried evolution of his musical ideas.

Shostakovich's chamber music has developed from the purely emotional to profound expression of suffering and resurrection, and in the latter phase fully reveals the significance of his achievement. His Quartet and Quintet were undoubtedly important contributions to Soviet chamber music. They have earned wide popularity and hold a firm place in the repertories of chamber music ensembles. These works, like the Fifth and Eighth Quartets of Myaskovsky, the "Slavic Quartet" of Shebalin, the Second Quartet of Prokofieff and the Pianoforte Trio of Khachaturyan display Soviet chamber music at its best. One may safely say that the String Quartet and Pianoforte Quintet of Dmitri Shostakovich belong to the best compositions of Soviet chamber music.

In 1939–1940 the composer's attention was held by another great task which he had set himself—the new orchestration of Mussorgsky's opera "Boris Godunov." As is known, this opera was long rendered as orchestrated by N. Rimsky-Korsakov. In 1927 the Stanislavsky Opera House in Moscow for the first time produced the opera in its original version. This was an important event in the musical life of the country. Some years later the original version of "Boris Godunov" was once more presented on the stage of the Bolshoi Opera House. Here it was found that Mussorgsky's orchestration, original and rich though it was, did not always satisfy the acoustic requirements of a large theatre hall. It was then realized that a fresh instrumentation of the opera would be necessary (that of Rimsky-Korsakov could no longer be used since it deviated considerably from the original, omitted entire scenes, etc.).

The task was finally assigned to Shostakovich who went to work with a will. His problem was not an easy one. He had to find the means of faithfully rendering the ideas of Mussorgsky while making fullest use of all the qualities of the modern symphonic orchestra. At the same time he had to assimilate the character of the music to avoid discrepancies of style. There were many who could not believe that a composer with so marked a musical individuality would be able to subordinate his own gifts to the faithful restoration of the work of an old master. His exceptional talent and love of Russian music enabled Shostakovich to cope with his task nonetheless. Just as the Bolshoi Opera House was preparing for its new production of "Boris Godunov," the war intervened and the score has remained in the composer's portfolio to this day.

CHAPTER VII

BORN OF THE STORM

In May 1941 Soviet composers and music critics gathered in Leningrad from all parts of the Soviet Union. A plenary session of the Soviet Composers' Union committees, convened here, dealt mainly with questions of symphonic music. At one of the concerts, the orchestra of the Leningrad Philharmonic gave a brilliant rendition of Shostakovich's Sixth Symphony under the baton of Eugene Mravinsky. The author was absent. He was in the south, in sunny Tbilisi, and never heard the heated discussions which once more flared up over his symphony. Much was said of the fate of the Soviet symphony, of its various schools and trends, of the necessity of creating an heroic symphony. None who participated in these discussions then dreamt that within a few months in this very city a grand symphonic poem dedicated to struggle would be written.

The circumstances under which the Seventh Symphony was written were unusual. "At the beginning of the war," relates the composer, "I volunteered for the Red Army, but was told to wait. I submitted a second application immediately after Stalin's speech referring to the people's volunteer forces. This time I was told: 'We'll accept you, but meanwhile go back and continue the work you've been doing.' The concert season ended and I began to receive my students again. Our studies continued until the first of July. I did not go on vacation, but spent my nights and days in the conservatory. Believing that they had forgotten about me, I submitted a third application to the People's Volunteer Forces. They had received very many applications such as mine. One was submitted by Professor Nikolayev who was 70 years old. Finally I was appointed to direct the musical activities of the People's Volunteer Force theatre. I'll write about that theatre some day. The artists of this theatre made frequent trips to the front, but it was difficult to direct its musical activities since its instruments consisted entirely of accordions. I soon renewed my requests to join the Red Army and was eventually received by a commissar. He listened to my request and then declared that it would be difficult to place me in the army. He was certain that I should continue to write music. I was released from the theatre of the People's Volunteer Force and, against my will, was to have been evacuated from Leningrad. I felt that I would be more useful here and had a serious talk about this with the directors. They insisted that I should leave, but I was in no hurry. The city's fighting spirit was superb. Housewives, children and the aged alike bore themselves manfully. I'll never forget the women of Leningrad who fought the fires and fire bombs. They were true heroines.

"As regards myself, I was a volunteer roof watcher of the conservatory.

"I began to work on the Seventh Symphony on the 19th of July and finished the third movement on September 29. My frame of mind was unusual. Three large movements— 52 minutes of music—were written very quickly and I was afraid that this would tell on the quality, that the symphony would reveal traces of haste. But my colleagues, who heard the music, were favorably impressed.

"I remember the dates very well. The first movement was finished on September 3, the second on September 17, and the third on September 29. I kept working by day and night. There were times when the anti-aircraft guns were in action and bombs were falling, but I kept working.

"On September 25 I celebrated my 35th birthday in Leningrad. I worked especially hard on that day and I have been told that that which I wrote on my birthday is particularly moving."

That is how the Seventh Symphony was written. Modest as always, the composer omitted to mention certain things. He did not mention the fact that in September hard fighting was already in progress at the very gates of the city which was being furiously shelled. . . . In spite of this, his work progressed rapidly. He did his duty as a Soviet composer courageously and staunchly.

On December 27, 1941, in Kuibyshev, Shostakovich for the first time played the score to his friends. "We entered a small, almost unfurnished room," related one of those present. "You could see that the apartment had only just been occupied, that no one had lived here for a long time. There was a piano, several chairs, a bed, and nothing more. Shostakovich arose to greet us.

"We hadn't seen him for a long time and exchanged brief accounts of our common acquaintances and friends. Shostakovich wanted to know if we had heard anything about his friend Leo Oskarovich Arnshtam, the cinema regisseur. I told him that Arnshtam had nearly lost his life in a recent automobile accident, but he scarcely heard what

I said. 'Yes, yes . . .' he murmured absently, and removing his jacket, he seated himself at the piano.

"It was only after he had finished playing, after he had received our congratulations and when we were drinking a toast to the new-born symphony that he suddenly approached me and asked with anxiety: 'What did you say happened to Arnshtam?' He wanted to hear the details of the accident, shook his head and murmured words of sympathy. He then snatched his hat and coat and ran off to send a telegram to Arnshtam.

"And so on the 27th of December, 1941, we first heard the composer play the score of his symphony. Sitting on the very edge of the piano stool, he was a lean, angular figure of a man, and in his suspenders and tuft-knobbed cap resembled a very well-behaved schoolboy. . . ."

In March 1942 the Seventh Symphony earned its composer the Stalin Prize, First Class. This was the second time he had won the prize. It was a second mark of appreciation from Soviet society. The composer then went to Moscow to attend the premiere of his Seventh Symphony. Here too he participated in the second All-Slav Congress. In a radio address he declared: ". . . Men and women of culture, science and art in our country are devoting all their energies to the struggle against fascism. Our scientists, writers, artists and composers are laboring with redoubled effort. They know what is at stake and we are happy in the certainty that our children and grandchildren, that our future generations will one day say: 'In those memorable days Russian culture, Russian science and Russian art rose to their full heights.' They produced wonderful inventions which helped the Red Army to fulfil its historic mission. They also produced wonderful inventions of art, memorials of the great struggle. It is this unity of Russian, Ukrainian, Belorussian, Polish, Czech, Slovakian, Croatian and Slovenian culture which has displayed the inherent qualities of the Slav peoples, their power of will and courage, their belief in themselves and their strength, their age-old noble striving to support all mankind in the struggle against the dark forces of the oppressors. . . ." In these words the composer revealed his understanding of the artist's mission in our times.

Shostakovich toured the Soviet Union in the spring and summer. After his Moscow triumphs he visited Novosibirsk where he met his old friends, the musicians of the Leningrad Philharmonic Orchestra. It was with great pleasure that he attended a performance of his Seventh Symphony by the orchestra under the baton of Eugene Mravinsky (who had been the first conductor to interpret his Fifth and Sixth Symphonies). Shostakovich departed from Novosibirsk in a happy frame of mind. This reunion with his old Leningrad friends had meant much to him.

September found him in Moscow again. Concerts of his music followed one upon the other. Presented to the public twice, the Seventh Symphony was very enthusiastically received on both occasions. The composer himself several times played the pianoforte score of his Quintet. A special evening was held in his honor in the Central Club of Artists. The affair was attended by the leading figures of Moscow's art world. Writers, artists, architects and musicians warmly greeted their favorite composer. Shostakovich then returned to Kuibyshev and in the winter of 1943 moved to Moscow with his family.

Today he resides and works in the Soviet capital. He is a professor of the Moscow Conservatory. An active figure in the Union of Soviet Composers, he is also a member of its organizational committee.

The first public performance of the Seventh Symphony was held in Kuibyshev on March 5, 1942. The splendid orchestra of the State Bolshoi Theatre under the baton of Samosud gave an excellent interpretation of the symphony. Present in the audience were eminent artists, scientists, representatives of the diplomatic corps, the Soviet and foreign press. The symphony then began its triumphant round of the concert halls of the Soviet Union. The Kuibyshev and Moscow presentations were followed by performances in Yerevan, Tashkent, Novosibirsk, Saratov, Sverdlovsk and other cities. The Seventh everywhere attracted wide attention. Red Army men, intellectuals, workers and office employees listened raptly to every measure and carried away with them something of the heroic spirit of Leningrad. Listening to the symphony, each had his own thoughts. Some were reminded of the November nights in Moscow, the capital on the alert, the sweeping beams of the searchlights, the thunder of the AA guns. Others thought of the great City of Lenin so stoutly defended by the people. Still others thought of the vast shops of factories and plants where the weapons of the Red Army were being forged. One and all, they were imbued with patriotism and boundless love of country.

When the Seventh Symphony was being performed in the decorous Hall of Columns of the Moscow House of Trade Unions, the composer was seated somewhere in the middle of the audience. He was surrounded by the people whose courage had inspired him to write the composition. Suddenly the wailing of the sirens pierced the stillness of the evening. The enemy's aircraft were trying to penetrate to the capital. The concert continued nonetheless. When the last, mighty chords had been sounded the people sprang from their seats to applaud the composer. At that moment a man appeared on the stage to warn the audience that an air alert had been sounded. No one left the hall. The people were completely under the spell of the music. The applause swelled to an ovation and Shostakovich, lanky and spectacled mounted the stage again and again.

Another memorable concert was held in November 1942, in Saratov, on the banks of the Volga. The city had already been touched by the breath of battle enveloping Stalingrad. Every bar of the symphony attained fresh significance, reminded the audience of the heroic defenders of the Volga citadel. In the audience there were many Red Army men who had just arrived from Stalingrad or were bound there the following morning.

When the concert was over the people did not disperse for a long time. Many mounted the stage to give vent to their feelings in words. A telegram of greetings was sent to the composer.

Shostakovich's new symphony was also well received abroad. Soon after its premiere, a number of leading men of music in the United States and Great Britain requested that they be sent the score as soon as possible. The long journey of the score was not untouched with romance. Recorded on microfilm, it was packed in a small tin and flown from Moscow to Teheran by plane. It then travelled for many miles by automobile and eventually reached Cairo. Flown over the yellow sands of the Sahara and the Atlantic wastes it finally reached the American continent. Foremost conductors vied with one another for the honor to be the first to render the symphony in the Western Hemisphere. Hundreds of thousands waited impatiently to hear this work which had been composed under such unusual circumstances. The symphony was first heard in New York where it was broadcast on July 19, 1942. The conductor was Arturo Toscanini. Subsequently it was conducted by Leopold Stokowski, by Serge Koussevitzky, by Rodzinski and others. The public was delighted and Shostakovich grew more popular than ever.

The composer found it necessary to offer a commentary on his work. In one of his articles he wrote: "The Seventh Symphony is a program composition inspired by the grim events of 1941. It consists of four movements. The first tells how our pleasant and peaceful life was disrupted by the ominous force of war. I did not intend to describe the war in a naturalistic manner (the drone of aircraft, the rumbling of tanks, artillery salvoes, etc.). I wrote no so-called battle music. I was trying to present the spirit and essence of those harsh events.

"The exposition of the first movement tells of the happy life led by the people, of their certainty in themselves and security for the future. It was a simple and peaceful life, such as was led by thousands of the Leningrad volunteer fighters before the war, such as was led by the entire city and the entire country. The theme of war governs the middle passages.

"The second movement is a lyrical Scherzo recalling times and events that were happy. It is tinged by a touch of melancholy.

"The third movement, a pathetic Adagio, expressing ecstatic love of life and the beauties of nature, passes uninterrupted into the fourth which, like the first, is a fundamental movement of the symphony. The first movement was expressive of struggle, the fourth, of approaching victory."

This program is presented vividly and with conviction. The content of the Seventh Symphony indeed is self-evident and evokes many sentiments and ideas scarcely touched upon in the literary exposition of its program. This is seen when analysing the music.

The first movement is the longest and itself occupies the entire first half of the concert. Introducing the fundamental idea of the symphony, it is expressive of conflict between the constructive and destructive forces, culture and barbarism, humanism and misanthropy. The composer's ideas cover an enormous orbit and this lends the work a monumental aspect. A large orchestra is required to preserve its grandeur, and the acoustic qualities of a large hall are imperative. Enlarged as far as possible, the orchestra numbers 80 strings instead of the usual 50 or 60. There are 8 French horns, 6 trumpets and 6 trombones.

The logic of this symphonic tale is well set off by its graphic metaphor and because of this the first movement, despite its complexity, is comprehensible to all. Though each listener is inclined to understand the music in his own way, its essence impresses itself most vividly. One would have to be utterly callous to art not to feel the atmosphere here created of the great struggle of the Soviet people in the summer and autumn of 1941. It is to this that the symphony owes its grandeur. As Alexei Tolstoi aptly put it: "Shostakovich rested his ear against the heart of his country and heard its mighty and magnificent song." It is to this (and not to ethnographic detail) that the work owes its national character and its claim to the heritage of the Russian classical traditions. This too lends the score its human significance, since the struggle of the Russian people, which inspired the composer, was also the cause of all progressive mankind. The national is here merged with the human element and therein lies the secret of the symphony's success abroad.

The symphony opens with a broad majestic theme. Its proud gait, bold melodic line and bright major character create a mood of courage and self-confidence—qualities which the composer justly attributed to the heroes of his symphony. It would be wrong, however, to regard this theme as a melodic portrait. The musical ideas only generalize the heroic character of the people. This is even more fully expressed in the development of the main theme.[1]

This development, as always the case with Shostakovich, is broad and free. As it becomes enriched by secondary voices, we are made constantly aware of new shades of meaning. Some of these new elements are especially significant. Even the brief melodic progress of D-C-B-B magically changes the flow of ideas. The same is true of an ascending scale passage stubbornly reiterated.

The second theme is a charming cantilena of violins against a rustling of violas and violoncellos. This is warm limpid music suggestive of idyllic calm, and peace with the world. Literary commentators have regarded this as expressing the happiness of the people. Such interpretation, of course, is not only feasible, but suitable to the ideas of the symphony as a whole and particularly so with regard to the first movement. This theme, however, seems of even greater

---

[1] In outline this theme is characteristic of Shostakovich's style. There is the familiar breadth of melody striding over a generous range of intervals. One may also perceive the diatonic intonations peculiar to him, though they are periodically interrupted by extraneous elements. Finally, there is his characteristic polyphony and texture.

import to me. With the preceding theme it creates a revealing portrait of our free Soviet man: not only his courage and fortitude, but his warm humanity, his natural poetic feeling, his aspiration towards a fine ideal. Though different from the first and main theme of the symphony, the second does not *oppose* the first, but rather *supplements* it. The impulse of the further development of the first movement therefore had logically to be furnished by an external element, something alien. The theme of war is thus not introduced merely as an item of the program, but owes its inception to psychological causes and the logic of the symphony's development. The program, as may be seen, did not serve Shostakovich as a prop (as it so often does for less gifted composers), but legitimately entered upon its own as an organic part of the general idea.

The new subject is comprised of two elements: the reiterated rhythm of the drum

and a crisp melody, rejecting, as it were, all that pertains to life with fateful automatic persistence. Those who are fond of drawing analogies might here discern something that is akin in spirit to the songs of the German soldiers. The rhythm of drums too reminds one of the German military marches. This matters little, however. Shostakovich was not striving for naturalistic effects (though this did not preclude individual strokes of descriptions). His idea went deeper. He confronts a vast world of human feelings with the bluntness and brutality of the modern Vandals.

One may safely say that the development of the symphony bears the stamp of genius. Its revelation of the enemy is a veritable *tour de force;* it awes us with its picture of titanic strife out of which comes the triumph of reason and justice. The theme of invasion enters as a sinister tattoo of the side-drum creeping into a tranquil flute and violin duet. We are reminded of Antokolsky's verse:

At an early morning hour, the best enjoyed by man,
When mothers fed their infants at the breast,
And life and song of daily work began,
And lowing cattle veiled the steppes in dust,
And children in their camps blew the reveille,
And the early thrush sang a pensive song—
When our country breathed peaceful abundance
In life, song and labour,
The enemy chose that peaceful summer dawn
To bomb our Soviet ports and towns.

At first hearing, the war theme seems just an odd little tune, unpretentious, even pedestrian and commonplace. But there is a snarl in this unexpected musical grimace which puts us on the alert. Stage by stage, as though by some inexorable schedule, the volume steadily increases, the theme goes marching on, rustling, rattling, shouting until it roars at us like a wild beast. And now it becomes a gigantic force which, it seems, nothing can stop. We recognize it now. This is the stride of a monster, inimical to all that lives and intent only upon mutilation and destruction.

Interesting is the fact that the composer here resorted to his old principles of the grotesque. Formerly, however, they served for the expression of the carefree jest, but now they have become a powerful means of description, a most effective method of depicting that genius of evil and those destructive forces which menaced the entire world, the whole of human progress and culture.

The means by which this effect was obtained are very simple and consist mainly in the automatic reiteration of the main melody and those of the secondary voices which cling to it as it progresses from phase to phase. The secondary voices, moreover, are merged into a flood of sound which, chaotic though it seems, preserves a certain order of its own. It is the order of a machine from hell geared for destruction. The secondary voices are various. At first there is the awkward strumming of fifths (E♭-B♭) in the lower register of the violoncellos. Then there is an ascending passage carried by double basses and violoncellos which at that juncture serves to heighten the stride of the main theme. Now added to this is the automatic reiteration of B♭-B♭-C-B♭ first carried by the violoncellos and then sounded with abruptness in the lower register of the piano. Constant repetition of this fragment (passing to the upper register of the violins and xylophone) with the growing volume of sound and unvarying rhythm create the impression of approaching masses of ponderous machinery. The music is enlivened then, but how terrible are the new voices. There are bestial groans (emitted by woodwind, string and French horn progressions of G, C, C-sharp and B♭) and heart-rending cries (produced by chromatic thirds). A great bell tolls over all. This avalanche of sound, the cries, shrieks and tocsin bell present a devastating impression of the fascist invasion.

Some critics have compared this passage with the famous "Bolero" of Ravel. The similarity, it seems to me, is merely of a superficial nature. There is the same repetition of rhythm and melody while the action is steadily mounting. In the Seventh Symphony, however, this attains altogether different meaning. Ravel's work presents a colorful picture of national festivity. His theme is charming and full of sensuous beauty. Gaining in lustre as it grows, it finally emerges in full splendor, a brilliant musical emblem of life. Shostakovich's theme, on the other hand, is soulless to the point of caricature. Gaining in horror as it grows, it finally confronts the listener with something that is starkly revolting. In addition to this, Shostakovich's theme gathers secondary voices in its stride, covert currents leading to psychological complication of the counterpoint. This is not true of the "Bolero," in which the counterpoint is purely ornamental.

. . . When the war theme reaches its culminating point it would seem that no forces on earth could stand up against its crushing weight and that everything human must go under. It would seem that the victory of barbarism and bestiality were inevitable. But in the storm of sound one suddenly hears the voices of French horns, trumpets and trombones, voices that are firm, sure and brave. Words will scarcely suffice to describe the daring and truthfulness of this sudden turn of musical thought. Few listeners can repress a sigh at that point when hope and even certainty of victory is reborn. A long and stubborn struggle lies ahead and the composer's consciousness of this shaped the further development of his symphony.

The new theme impresses itself strongly upon the listener because it is simple, clear and easy to remember. Its melodic prototype was invoked (by a descending progression of D-C-B-B) when the main theme was presented. This connection is psychologically justified. That which is barbarous is confronted with the humane and the mechanical forces are checked by a wall of courage and selfless heroism. The melodic lines of the theme here and there recall certain of the most popular songs of the Soviet people and this renders it even more comprehensible and dear to them.

The opposing forces stand face to face. At first powerfully proclaimed in unison by the brass, the theme is reiterated by trumpets and trombones against a background of agitated violins and woodwind. The drums maintain the rhythm of their march and once more everything seems to hang in the balance, but the first theme of the symphony rises determinedly and the grim spectre recedes to the background.

The main theme appears in a minor key, and acquires severity and determination. Human dignity has been outraged by the sanguinary visions of war. However the sentiment is not one of fear or confusion, but of self-sacrifice and unbending will for struggle. The action of the music is intensified. That which at first appeared in a proud, lofty vein and was expressive of the people's serenity and certainty in their strength, is now set in motion. The composer has accomplished this by introducing fresh elements of activity and new polyphonic undercurrents.

The second theme is transformed to an even greater degree. After great trials and suffering it is not easy at once to recall unclouded happiness. The even rustling of the strings which sounded idyllic in the exposition now receives a sorrowful shading (emphasized dissonance), the formerly bright refrain of the flutes is touched with sorrow. The melody is picked up by the clarinet and grows softer until

116

all is still and only the pulsating chords of the string and piano continue the train of thought. The solemn low register of the bassoon then introduces one of the most moving passages.

This passage was perhaps best described by the writer Eugene Petrov when he said: "It is a march commemorating those who fell for their country, but it evokes no tears. Its grief is too deep for tears—a mark of weakness. No, this is no time for a display of weakness. There must be no weakness, not for a moment, not for a second. And this requiem to our heroes, to our brothers, sons and fathers leaves us dry-eyed but with fists clenched." The grief of brave men is here set forth with classical simplicity. The melody seems limitless in its expression of loss and urgings for revenge. No less than brilliant are its final bars. The sorrowful refrain suddenly gives way to the bright and warm second, lyrical theme, which, as it were, recalls the happy past of those who laid down their lives for their country. The composer now returns to the main theme of his symphony, serene and soft, though sounded by full and generous chords. Even more calm is the brief reiteration of the second theme. Nearly pellucid is the final melody of the violins and the reserved gait of violoncellos and double basses. . . . The distant drubbing of the drums is here followed by a muted and sombre repetition of the war theme.

Great artist that he is, Shostakovich possesses a fine sense of proportion and this too was shown in his Seventh Symphony. He does not return to his description of the enemy presented in the music of the first movement. Henceforth he devotes himself to the expression of his ideal of humanism. He unfolds the sentiments of the free man and describes his exultation over coming victory. Though complementing the first movement, the three last movements thus pass into other spheres of emotion.

The Scherzo offers an unexpected contrast to the tension of the first movement. The composer himself has referred to the Scherzo as "very lyrical," and it is truly pervaded by the lyrical rather than by the playful and humorous principle. It is as graceful and colorful as the best of Shostakovich's works of this nature, but its soulful lyricism has not been equalled by any Scherzo he has written hitherto.

The Scherzo of the Seventh possesses that lyricism and lightness which reminds one of many melodies of Tchaikovsky. The analogy arises of itself. There is no resemblance in style, of course. The theme is characteristic of Shostakovich and true to his melodic and somewhat angular vein. The similarity rests rather with its emotional content, its almost pellucid melancholy, clarity of outlook and moral soundness. The gentle sorrow of the Scherzo does not sadden the listener. Full of poetic charm, it reminds him of the simple beauty of the Russian landscape and the gentle lyricism of the old Russian songs. Tchaikovsky and Shostakovich, therefore, derived inspiration from a single source, and this accounts for a certain relation in the nature of their melodies. Most remarkable is the fact that Shostakovich, whose melodies have so often evoked a smile, has written a theme wherein grace and subtle humor are tinged with melancholy, and which is so deeply permeated with emotion, heartfelt and warm.

The theme of the Scherzo, too, attests to the evolution of a composer who has been seeking to render his music comprehensible to all. Shostakovich's works are complex, of course, and not by any means accessible to the untrained

118

ear; but the appearance in his compositions of new, well-defined themes, which cling to the memory at a first hearing, shows that he has assimilated the traditions of the classic symphony. History has shown that it was only when richness of content and skill of polyphonic treatment was matched with clarity and comprehensibility of melody that symphonic music earned general recognition and understanding.

A detailed analysis of the Scherzo is scarcely necessary. One could dwell upon its individual subjects that alternate so fancifully. One could discuss the score in detail and once more convince oneself of the skill of the composer's instrumentation, the subtlety and richness of his polyphony. This would lead to a repetition of much that has been said before, since there is much in the Scherzo that is reminiscent of its predecessors. This too attests to the maturity of the composer whose methods have progressed logically from composition to composition (not in the sense that they were merely repeated, but in that they were invariably marked by that flexibility and freedom characteristic of his work). It shows too that the die of his style has been cast, that his music has gained that quality by which the works of one composer are distinguished from those of another.

The next phase of the symphony is its stately Largo. In one of his articles Shostakovich wrote that he had here meant to express "ecstatic love of life and the beauties of nature." These sentiments are indeed most effectively expressed by the Largo. The vistas of its melodic current are boundless. A wealth of sentiment, reflections of human happiness and liberty found expression here.

Other works of the composer too contained the profound Largo, but pervaded with pathos, sorrow and tragedy. The Largo of the Seventh, on the other hand, is a musical embodiment of clairvoyant human thought. Only a pure and fiery spirit could have erected such a monument of music to that which is noble and honorable in the nature of man. The breadth and tide of its emotion bring it near to such classics of the Russian symphony as the Andante of Tchaikovsky's Fifth Symphony and the slow movements of Scriabin's Second and Third Symphonies, whose traditions it unquestionably shares. Again and again one perceives the connection between the music of Shostakovich and that of the great Russian masters.

A salient feature of the Largo is the continuity of its melodic current. Few contemporary composers are capable of such freedom in development of melody. Extraordinarily long, the Largo contains a series of passages expressive of all the sentiments which moved the composer to the creation of this symphony.

The Largo is introduced by a mighty chorale, captivating for its solemn chords and the severe diatonic progression of the basses. This leads to a vibrant unison of the violins, voicing one of the principal motifs of the Largo, a penetrating melody at once active and raptly profound. The chorale is sounded again. The melodic progression of the basses is emphasized and evokes a more determined reply from the violins. This first passage of the Largo recalls the Bach "Inventions." Shostakovich here united the abstract with the concrete, philosophical meditation with sensuous beauty of sound.

An exceptionally serene melody is voiced in the background by the high register of a flute. The composer was justified when he said that the Largo expressed ecstatic love for nature. Only meditation over the beauty of the world could prompt such a melody, akin alike to the quiet of a summer evening, to the green gloaming of the woods, to the blue of the seas and the skies. Such a view may seem subjective. Perhaps so, but far be it from me to force it upon anyone. Nor will I try to prove that the Largo depicts this or that specific scene in nature. But if one should seek for something more in music than a mere weave of melodic lines, if one should try to determine just what human sentiment is closest to this serene melodic current surely no objections will be offered to such an attempt at fathoming the secrets of the composer's train of thought.

The solo flute is soon joined by a second in a lower register and this is somewhat reminiscent of the Largo in the Fifth Symphony. The theme is repeated in a briefer version as modified by the strumming of violoncellos whose swinging gait sets another current flowing against the background of the introductory chorale, now presented softly and restrained by prolonged chords of the strings and the ringing of a harp. The austere melody of the violins rises again, but a scale-like passage descending from its peak note (A of the fourth octave) emphasizes, as it were, the quiet that follows. In the place of the serene concluding cadenzas that might have been expected at this point, there begins a recharging of rhythmic energy. A new episode, determined and purposeful, now comes to the fore.

Against the background of syncopated chords, executed by violas and French horns, the violins bear a proud melody. Bold and angular, it surges persistently forward. Its crisp rhythm and brisk motion, the even pulsations of its accompaniment and energy of its attendant undercurrents lends it a dynamic quality contrasting the pensive cantilena of the flutes. The sweeping spirit of the passage is concentrated in an imperious melody of the French horns,

attended by sharp rhythmic chords of the strings and gives rise finally to the solemn chorale.

The commencement of the chorale is truly grand. Shostakovich here makes the most of the brass. The lower current is carried by two trombones, a tuba, a bass-clarinet, a bassoon, a double bassoon and double bass. The continuity of rhythm introduces a new element into the chorale. Effectively merged at this point is the grandeur of the first and the determined progression of the second passage of the Largo. Similarly impressive is the broad unison of the violins endowed with even greater activity owing to the same continuity of melody. The E-major cantilena of the flutes once more floats to the surface at the end. It is presented more quietly and peacefully here owing to the chords of the harp relieving the dry *pizzicato* of the strings, and the rich middle register of the viola which intones the main theme. The woodwinds softly repeat the *pizzicato* chords of the strings three times and this terminates the splendid musical poem. The listener is thus carried away from the terrible scenes of the first movement by the tender melancholy and subtle humor of the Scherzo, and the austere meditation and solemn pathos of the Adagio. The human ideal is unfolded in all its grandeur and beauty. But the struggle is not yet over and this is recalled by the restless introduction of the Finale.

The Finale is no less grandly conceived, no less varied in content than the first movement. It once more reflects the fury of battle, revives the declamatory pathos of the Adagio and finally presents a dazzling vision of victory. It differs from the first movement in that the composer here omits the grisly image of the enemy. The active principle prevailing in the Finale lends it the character of an epic poem of struggle crowned with a radiant and exulting final passage.

Returning abruptly to the motif of struggle after the respite offered by the second and third movements, the Finale is introduced by muted violoncellos and double basses. There is the distant ominous drubbing of the kettle-drums and an agitated phrase carried by the violins. The restlessness of the introductory passage recalls the conclusion of the first movement where the theme of war was last sounded.

The uneasy character of the first pages of the Finale is expressively emphasized by the violoncellos and double basses (which play a primary role throughout), the oboes and French horns which sound like signals for battle. Though the principal subjects are anticipated here, no definite course has yet been adopted.

But finally the theme is found in a determined phrase of the violoncellos and double basses. The melody now surges irresistibly forward. Bold and swift, its energy is contagious. New melodies appear, but they are allied closely with the introductory subject. So are the crisply rhythmic chords of the strings and brasses, fascinating for their daring up-grade stride. So, too, is the vigorous canon based on the introductory measures of the main theme (constantly drifting to the surface and knitting the manifold passages into a single, well-shaped whole). At the culminating point, against pulsating gusts of trumpet and trombone chords, there is an angry downward rush of scales which revive the theme, now more determined in character owing to its stronger rhythmic impulse

A restrained moderato then introduces a section permeated with sorrow and recalling the requiem of the bassoon at the end of the first movement. The greater severity and restraint are here reminiscent of the solemn chorale in the Adagio. The music proceeds in the gait of a sarabande. Owing to continuous progression of melody its sorrowful vein gives way to a sterner one of courage and action. Some parts here are unforgettable. It is sufficient to mention those measures wherein the first violin sorrowfully invokes the main theme against a background of violoncellos and violas, creating an atmosphere of profound grief. This is a good example of melody transformation peculiar to the symphonic works of Shostakovich. The outlines of the main theme grow steadily clearer and the constant intensification of the action anticipates the exultant final pages of the symphony. Of significant philosophical import is the fact that the composer passes to triumph from pathos and sorrow. His thoughts of victory are bound with the memory of those who laid down their lives for liberty. That pathos too lends particular radiance to the final and triumphant passage. The brevity of the latter is more impressive than many a wordier symphonic Finale. The conclusion of the Seventh Symphony palpitates with life. Arisen from ardent hope of ultimate triumph, it expresses unwavering certainty of final victory.

How does Shostakovich deal with his motif of imminent victory? For this he avails himself of altered versions of his principal motifs, the main theme of the first movement and the theme of the Finale (to be more exact, its vigorous introductory intonation). The victory theme is woven from the heroic subjects expressive of the free and proud human consciousness, and the themes of intense action. The composer thus identifies victory with the most exalted strivings of mankind and at the same time indicates the only path by which these strivings can be realized—the path of severe and relentless struggle.

Both themes are mightily sounded by the brass instruments. The effect of exultation is here emphasized by the swift pace of undercurrents, by frequent repetitions of the latter and this lends the whole a stirring and festive nature. Nothing new to Shostakovich, this method is closely allied to his favorite principle of checking the flight of his rhythm and of lending an automatic quality to the action of his themes. I may add that this method of ornamenting a theme by a repetition of joyous and palpitating intonations (applied with equal success by the composer in the Finales of his Fifth and Sixth Symphonies) is based on the traditions of the Beethoven Symphony. An example may be found in the final passage of the "Egmont" Overture where the mighty main theme is graced by a reiterated subject of the flute.

The symphony concludes with the final theme of the Finale carried by a bass-clarinet, a bassoon, a double bassoon, French horns, five trombones, a tuba, violoncellos and double basses. Nothing is permitted to impede the flow of the theme here. The polyphonic currents have been extinguished. Only the melodic progression remains and this is accentuated by buoyant gusts of an organ until relieved by

major chords in the high registers of the strings, woodwinds, trumpets and French horns. The theme leads for
the last time to the thunder of kettledrums, and brilliant
major chords bring the great symphonic poem of struggle
and victory to a close.

The contents of the Seventh Symphony are so well
defined that differences of opinion are scarcely likely. It
would not do, however, to oversimplify the meaning. This
symphony of Shostakovich is an embodiment both of the
hero of our times and the pathos of his great struggle. Shostakovich shared the thoughts and sentiments of his people
and this accounts for the range of the symphony—from
stern courage to tender lyricism, from drollery to philosophic meditation.

This wealth of sentiment is contrasted by something
fearfully limited, deadly mechanistic, soullessly brutal.
When the symphony was written the forces of progress
and reaction, Democracy and Fascism, were locked in combat and Shostakovich strove to embody the world tragedy
of war in his music.

But this is not the only significance of the symphony.
If this alone were true then Shostakovich's Seventh would
have been a story of contemporary life in general and not
necessarily of Soviet contemporary life. Actually, its composition was prompted by the grim events of 1941, by the
heroic struggle of the Soviet people and it therefore mainly
expresses the sentiments and ideas of these people. This can
be felt in the patriotic spirit which pervades the symphony
and the composer's philosophic generalisation of definite
facts from our history. He reminds his listeners of one
cloudless Sunday morning, when the quiet was shattered by
fascist tanks. He reminds them of the staunch courage of

our people, of their sorrow for the fallen and their joyous anticipation of victory. His motifs have been ours, things that we have experienced and suffered, and the Seventh Symphony for that reason is primarily a story of the Russian, the Soviet people.

The chief merit of a work of art, prompted by the most progressive ideas of its time, however, is that it knows no barriers and is comprehensible to all honest men regardless of nationality. This symphonic story of the defenders of the Soviet Land was warmly received by all who sympathized with their great and sacred struggle.

The Seventh Symphony was a logical phase of Shostakovich's development. It was prompted, of course, by history and would never have appeared in its present aspect in times of peace. Its philosophical trend and style, however, are closely linked with the evolution of Shostakovich's art. Its lofty moral message and humanistic ideals reveal on a higher plane those qualities which were already observed in the Fifth Symphony and Pianoforte Quintet. The hero of the Seventh, moreover, is the hero of the Fifth Symphony who has now run an ordeal of suffering and doubt which he has conquered and has come to maturity. The tragic genre of the Seventh too is related to that of the Fifth. Though the composer's ideals and emotions are not limited to tragedy alone, his later works indicate that he has the gift of a great tragedian. This was manifested by the Seventh Symphony.

Much will undoubtedly be written about the Seventh Symphony, which will go down in the history of culture as a vital and artistic document of the struggle of a great people. Those who are at all receptive to music will recognize this story about a people whose brave struggle won happiness for all mankind, as an exalted work of art, morally pure and deeply human. To the composer, his Seventh Symphony will always represent one of his finest achievements at the apex of his talent.

This could conclude the chapter on the Seventh Symphony, but I should like to add a few words about those more modest compositions of Shostakovich which were written in immediate proximity to the Seventh. Such is the song for chorus, "Oath to the People's Commissar," a march for brass band, and the suite for chorus and orchestra called "To My Native Leningrad," written specially for a song and dance ensemble. The suite is comprised of five parts: the "October 1917 Overture," based on the melodies of all Revolutionary songs ("Warszawjanka" and "We're all of the People!"), "Dance of the Youth," orchestrated with the usual Shostakovich color, "Song of the Neva," "Song of Leningrad" and the broad musical monologue written to the words of the late Jambul, patriarch of Kazakh folk poesy. All these are akin in spirit to the Seventh Symphony (though immeasurably smaller in scale) and all attest to the fiery patriotism of the composer. In this, Shostakovich shares the sentiments of all Soviet composers. Each of them has been serving the cause of the people in proportion to his respective ability. This has been the source of patriotic songs, ballads, cantatas, operas and symphonies in the Soviet Union and these have forcefully expressed the grim spirit and grandeur of our times. A leading place among such compositions belongs to Shostakovich's Seventh Symphony of struggle and victory, a great work that was born of the storm.

CHAPTER VIII

CONCENTRATED THOUGHT
AND FEELING

Shostakovich spent the summer of 1943 at the "Creative Home" of the Union of Soviet Composers, near the city of Ivanovo. It was here, in the midst of a typical Russian rural setting, that he wrote his Eighth Symphony. Its premiere was given in Moscow, on November 4, 1943. Eugene Mravinsky, the old friend of the composer, the first to conduct the Fifth and Sixth Symphonies, again held the baton. Shostakovich dedicated the score of the Eighth to this prominent Soviet conductor, who now directs the symphonic orchestra of the Leningrad Philharmonic.

By its contents the Eighth Symphony is closely related to the Seventh, being a similar grandiloquent tale of our times. But the two works are at the same time profoundly different. If the Seventh can be called a monumental symphonic drama, the Eighth is a majestic tragedy. The flow of its musical thoughts is extraordinarily wide, Bach-like in the exalted and limitless slow motions. One must possess an out-of-the-common feeling for musical perspective to survey in one's mind the whole pattern of the tonal architecture, and to be able to deduct from the slowly developing chain of melodies the tense sensations which gave birth to this music.

The theme of struggle dominates in the Seventh Symphony; here the composer unfolds the tale of war's tragedy and hardships. Before his eyes there arise the ruins of destroyed cities, each loss is echoed in his suffering soul. And thus is originated a music which is cruel in its frankness, as frightening as the truth which gave birth to it. But the composer has other visions as well: courageous and energetic rhythms break into the flow of music, which now contains not only sobs and moans, but daring appeals as well—not only the numbness of grief, but the activity of struggle. The dramatic collisions of the symphony are concluded by the coming of a great light. As though after the bloody days of war there appears the dawn of coming victory. . . .

The conception of the symphony is clearly expressed by the juxtaposition of its separate parts—the exalted Adagio, the march-like Allegretto, the frantic Presto, the mournful Passacaglia and the luminous Finale. There sounds in this music a passionate humanitarian accusation, a flaming protest against fascist barbarity. It was written at the time of heavy combats, when Soviet men were pursuing the retreating enemy and with heavy hearts discovering the whole depth of the disaster inflicted by the aggressors. This feeling is reproduced with a strength of artistic conviction that makes the Eighth Symphony one of the most brilliant achievements of modern musical art.

The construction and structure of the Eighth are very complicated, and can serve as the theme of special theoretical study. The first thing that strikes one when studying the score is the paradoxical union of vastness of proportions and gargantuan scales with the finesse of details. The symphony reminds one of a cyclopic building which on closer examination shows a filigranic treatment of architectural details. Yet such is the strength of the composer's talent that this abundance of details does not lead to spottiness: they blend into severe lines which mark the noble contour of the symphonic construction. In a purely musical sphere this is expressed in the form of broad musical lines, that leave the impression of endless development, and at the same time—of the enormous expressive force of short phrases which appear and disappear unexpectedly. The unexpectedness of their appearance is merely apparent: for in fact each trait in them is logically justified and necessary to the embodiment of the composer's conception. This is in general typical of Shostakovich's creative power. But in none of his preceding works has this been so clearly expressed as in this voluminous score.

The first movement of the Symphony, the Adagio, is slow and severe. It is remarkable in its lofty unhurriedness of expression. It is an epic of great passions and majestic thoughts. The Adagio brilliantly displays that very quality of Shostakovich's talent which some critics denied him—the intensity of the melodic flow, the mastery of secret singing, in a word the quality that brings him close to the great Russian classics. An extraordinary gift of melodic development is necessary to hold the listener's attention so commandingly for a most serious and profound half-an-hour adagio.

If it were necessary to characterize the Adagio by a single phrase, the best way to describe it would be a symphonic song, full of the feelings of grief and sorrowful loss. "The victories owing to which the kingdoms of the aggressors, and empires of flame, iron and steel are crumbling to pieces, cannot be gained without profound suffering; and

131

following the heavy ringing steps of war the most natural sounds of the beat of millions of human hearts make themselves heard"; these words of Boris Assafyev, member of the Soviet Academy, apply best of all to the first part of the Symphony. The sensitive listener will catch the beat of millions of hearts, the suffering they lived through, in the calm flow of the mournful song, in the unexpected outbreak of an awe-inspiring storm of cries, wails and moans, and in the thought expressed by the coda, which is extraordinary in its concentration and expressiveness.

Highly characteristic of Shostakovich is the organic quality of shape, which is never schematized and is always new, always inseparably connected with the various artistic problems that arise in his consciousness. Thus in the Adagio of the Eighth everything is subjected to the principle of development. Therefore it contains scarcely any exact repetitions dictated by schemes. When he returns to some musical figure, the composer examines it in the light of the dramatic climaxes he has himself lived through, and adds to it new traits of expressiveness. To the attentive listener, the music of the Adagio opens a whole world of human sensations, expressed sincerely and truthfully.

We have already mentioned the singing quality of the Adagio. The melodic movement indeed becomes the dominating principle here. Its significance is underlined by dramatic episodes which bring in the necessary element of contrast. The elements of drama are already laid down in the introductory theme, which is built (as in the Fifth) on the contrasting juxtaposition of melodic elements. The wonderful artistic quality of the melodic development is apparent from the very first bars—the rise to a peak and the return to the point of departure. The singing of the violins against the background of regularly pulsating strings is even more impressive. For it is here that the composer attains an extraordinary length of melodic breathing and at the same time an extreme simplicity of exposition, in which there is not a single superfluous detail, not a single embellishment. It is the indivisible domination of a severe and concentrated thought. One typical detail is worthy of note: when it becomes necessary to bring variations into the technique, the composer introduces polyphonic elements—an oft-repeated simple, but significant phrase which further on unfolds melodically until it replaces the basic theme for a certain length of time. This is a very interesting example of Shostakovich's symphonic manner of thinking, for which the maximum utilization of the possibilities of the thematic material is typical. In his other works Shostakovich never introduces superfluous thematic material into the score; each musical idea unfolds and finds its place in the general structure. Herein lies the secret of the union between monumentality and minutely worked-out details. To Shostakovich, details are not ornaments, but necessary components of the structure.

The freely flowing song of the violins is touching and mournful. The calm current of the music is interrupted by a sudden medley of wild shrieks, cries and moans. The howling of the woodwinds is terrifying; there is something so soulless and cruel in the markedly rhythmical episode of the "allegro non troppo," in which the intonations of the introductory theme are irrecognizably transformed. The whole widely unfolded episode leaves the impression of a diabolical incantation, that grows like an avalanche and leads to the principal theme, which is carried through with great power. The methods of development which the composer applies here are exceptionally interesting and original. They are based on the introduction of new elements and the growing expressiveness of the music.

Probably the most striking moment of the Adagio is when the mighty *tutti* is replaced by the tremolo of the strings (*sfpp subito*) against the background of which is heard the elegiac melody of the English horn. This is one of those famous instrumental recitatives in the mastery of which Shostakovich has no rival amongst modern composers. It is the tensest moment of the drama, expressed in severely simple musical images. Then comes the decisive break in the symphonic narrative, which ends in the calm and limpid vibration of the strings (particular color being given by the harmonics of the first violins) and of the trumpet solo (*pp morendo*). All that has been experienced seems to retreat into the distance, and calm is established. However it is not the final solution of the dramatic climaxes, but merely the summing up of one cycle of meditations. The listener will still have to live through a lot, together with the composer, before the Finale of the grand symphonic epopee is reached.

The Adagio is followed by two movements, the Allegretto and the Allegro non troppo, which differ from it sharply both in the manner of execution and in the character of the music. They are dominated by determined rhythm and dynamic motion. The composer attains a graphic clarity of images, a sharpness of chiaroscuros which are in contrast to the cantilena of the Adagio. They give a new impulse to the symphonic unfolding, which had seemingly exhausted itself already in the first part of the Symphony, in which apparently everything had been fully exposed and brought to a logical conclusion.

The second and third movements are united by the common role assigned to them in the symphonic cycle. In the Allegretto the movement develops on two different planes: the clarity of somewhat coarse intonations, and the acuity of the grotesques. The second movement is brilliantly written, but is far inferior to the third, in which the composer has given expression to something quite new, and done so with striking forcefulness.

The score of this movement is a pure delight for the real music lover, with its astonishing simplicity and the frugality of its means of expression. But at the same time it surprises the listener by the novelty of its sonorities and the originality of its musical images. From the first bar to the last it is dominated by an uninterrupted even motion of fourths, that does not cease for a single instant. There is something deeply oppressive in it, there is something cruel and inhuman in its very automaticity. It is a kind of frightening "toccata of death," a diabolical *danse macabre*, an orgy of destructive barbaric forces. Against the background of this uninterrupted movement sound the harsh, abrupt chords of the strings and the terrifying shrieks of oboes and clarinets. The coloring of the trumpet solo is ominous, as it alternates with the harsh parallel fifths of the altos and first violins. The vision of a monstrous battlefield seems to unfold before us—a battlefield pockmarked with shell-holes, with bullets whistling overhead and shells exploding. The tenseness and sharpness of this music are tremendous. It inflicts a strong nervous reaction on the listener: consciousness is stunned by the continuity of the dynamic movement, the senses are overwhelmed by inhuman images so deftly called up by the composer. And after this startling picture of the fury of evil forces there follows, with indomitable logic, the embodiment of a people's grief —the stately and mournful passacaglia.

The Passacaglia (Largo) sounds like a funeral march, full of sorrow for the countless victims who perished; but of a sorrow which is stern and virile, which leaves the eyes dry and the fists clenched. There is no darkness of despair in this music, it is a concentration of deep feeling and indomitable will. At the same time it contains a real tenderness, which is all the more impressive because it shimmers through the severity and decisiveness of the melodic movement of the passacaglia. I even consider that in concentration of feeling and austere majesty of ideas this part of the symphony is superior to the remarkable introductory Largo. In modern art, tragedy very often assumes the form of superfluous expressiveness, which sometimes becomes affectation. But here Shostakovich attains the true simplicity of tragic expression. And the composer is quite right: the great suffering inflicted by war can only be told in such simple, human words as these.

The precise rhythmic theme of the Passacaglia is first introduced by a powerful unison of the whole orchestra. Over eight bars there is a *diminuendo* from FFF to P. Then the theme is repeated eleven times more in the bass (by the violoncellos and the double basses in octaves). On this foundation the composer keeps building up one new structure of tonalities after the other. Each new voice is full of deep significance, and develops the composer's idea further and further. It is difficult to say which is more impressive— the expressiveness of the melody or the finesse of the orchestral coloring. The recitatives of the flute solo, interrupted by tremolo chords on three flutes, penetrate the listener's consciousness particularly deeply. In these moments it seems

136

that all around everything has grown still, and that in the ensuing silence you can distinctly hear the beat of your heart. I know no other modern composer who can thus compel the listener to lend an attentive ear to silence, as Shostakovich does.

The severe and mournful character of the Largo is sustained right through. It contains no contrasts, the same idea unfolding wider and wider, and considerably emphasizing its meaning. In the end the mournful mood reaches its culmination, the shadows grow heavier and it seems that there can be no resolution. And then suddenly a miracle occurs—for one cannot call the imperious change of thought, brought about with a simplicity that amounts to genius, anything less than a miracle. It leads us out to the open, sunlit spaces of the Finale.

The chords of the three flutes have just sounded. . . . The clarinets start in low, and inspired. There is a hardly perceptible shift, and the grim Gb minor is replaced by the radiant C-major. A bass clarinet intones the tierce of the major triad, and it is as though a ray of light disperses the surrounding darkness.

The finale begins simply and unpretentiously with the light cantilena of the bassoon, supported by the only very slightly indicated accompaniment (second bassoon and contra-bassoon in octave). Then the woodwinds cede their place to the strings; further on, the flute introduces a graceful cantilena, and episode after episode of the musical story unfolds until the monumental epic poem is over.

The problem presented by the finale is one of the most complicated ones that a composer can have to solve in creating a symphonic cycle. To give a solution to all the dramatic climaxes is extremely difficult, and particularly in such a symphony as Shostakovich's Eighth. But the composer has brilliantly solved these difficulties. It is not merely that the introduction of the Finale comes at precisely the right moment and is so convincing, nor that the transition to new melodic material is in itself a masterpiece. The chief point is the psychological foundation of this music, which gives actual, not merely formal, solutions to the conflicts of the symphonic development.

In some respects the Finale of the Eighth is similar to that of the Piano Quintet. In both cases there comes an unexpected enlightenment, there unfolds a sunlit perspective, the radiance of which disperses the dark shadows of the past. But there is a basic difference between these two Finales: the dramatic collisions in the Symphony are immeasurably greater than those in the Quintet, and therefore the Finale of the Symphony is more multiform and more significant.

Some critics have reproached Shostakovich for the alleged superficiality of this symphonic finale. It seems to us that, on the contrary, it is full of a deep philosophic significance. What could the composer have juxtaposed to the limitless sea of human suffering, the story of which he told in the preceding movements of the symphony, if not this clarity, this bloom of a new life which conquers death and blossoms out with unrestrainable force? When, after the concluding hopelessly gloomy bars of the Passacaglia, the first major chord of the Finale is introduced and the bassoon starts its unpretentious little song, it seems as though green branches push their way upwards towards the sun from under the ruins—a symbol of the inexhaustible forces of life. If it is permissible to try to express the composer's idea in words, then it would seem to us that he wanted to express in sounds the unyielding faith that lived in the hearts of millions and helped them to exist through the blood and suffering. And one thing more—the passionate, deeply human dream of the future happiness of mankind, for which the peace-loving nations entered into mortal combat against fascism. In the remarkable coda of the Finale, in the clarity of the major harmonies, in the calmness of the diminishing melodic phrases, there is expressed a sensation of such purity, freshness and peacefulness as seemed lost forever and completely suppressed by the tragic—sometimes cruel —music of the first four movements of the Symphony. In listening to those movements one might have expected any conclusion—the catastrophe of annihilated consciousness or the triumph of victory—but never this radiant and harmonic solution to the climaxes. And if, despite its unexpectedness, the Finale succeeds in being convincing, then the composer has attained that very catharsis, which the ancient aesthetes considered a necessary attribute to true tragedy.

The Finale stresses the optimism of Shostakovich's symphonic tragedy. The work is characteristic of its country and its time in that it is penetrated by the spirit of tremendous activity, and that all the dramatic happenings cannot hide the final goal of the great struggle from the composer's vision. Shostakovich wrote his symphony in response to human grief and suffering, but not to plunge into an abyss of all-absorbing sorrow. He created a monument to the sufferings of millions, so that future generations should remember the price with which their happiness and freedom were bought. If his Seventh Symphony is to remain as a musical monument to the titanic struggle of the Soviet people against the foe, then in the music of the Eighth our descendants will hear the story of those inhuman sufferings, to forget which would be treason to the memory of those who fought and died in the great cause of liberation. Such is the objectively philosophic meaning of Dmitri Shostakovich's remarkable Eighth Symphony.

It is not so easy to penetrate the composer's conception. The Eighth belongs to the number of those artistic creations, the significance of which cannot be at once fully recognized, which demand a considerable intellectual effort for their perception. It is very complicated both in contents and in language. But the Eighth deserves such unusual concentration of attention, and to those who can penetrate its meaning, the Symphony has an unusual amount to say. It is a striking human document, a saga of difficult and glorious times.

It is the quintessence of a great composer's art, the art of a composer who disposes with assurance of all modern methods of musical expression, and has mastered the unattainable art of achieving tonalities, unexpectedly novel and acute, by utilizing the most simple—and apparently customary—means. It is necessary to stress this trait of Shostakovich's talent over and over again.

I want to point out another aspect of the orchestral score of the Eighth Symphony: namely, the unusual clarity and the delimitation of functions entrusted to separate instruments or groups of instruments. This increases the emotional effect of the music and also facilitates the perception of it. In addition there is the finesse of the melodic and harmonic languages. The composer makes a strict choice of the means of expression which are necessary to him, and works out each detail thoroughly, discarding everything that is superfluous. This transforms his music into a concentrate of thought and feeling, and gives it an extraordinary power of conviction.

Shostakovich's music is novel and highly original. Yet at the same time it is natural in the flow of its ideas. Everything in it is subjugated to a clearly thought-out conception, and every detail of it has a concrete significance. Any harmonic consonance or cunning contrapuntal combination of voices is the necessary form of expressing this conception. That is why his music appeals even to those who do not particularly appreciate the harsh consonances of modern musical language. Shostakovich's mastery of such details is perfect. However it is still more important to stress his exclusive mastery in the use of those means of musical expression, the secret of which seemed to have been lost by modern composers. By this are meant the clear diatonic harmonies, the frequent tonal colorings of classical music. This daring and convincing use of the classical creative heritage is one of the most interesting traits of Shostakovich's magnificent talent, which unfurls in all its power in the monumental Eighth Symphony.

The theme of the Eighth was also developed by Shostakovich in the sphere of chamber music, namely in the trio for piano, violin and violoncello which he wrote in the summer of 1944 and dedicated to the memory of his friend, the noted Soviet connoisseur of music Ivan Sollertinsky. The listener's attention is already fixed by the first bars. The timbre of the coloring is quite unusual: harmonics of the violoncello, combined with the sonorities of the violin's lower register. The singing melody, typically Russian in the intonation and register of its construction, is touching by its pure and delicate mournfulness. The breadth and significance of the melodic development are typical. The melody seems to push back the limits of the bars, giving birth to strange alternations in meter. However, this is only perceptible to the eye—the ear accepts it as quite natural.

The second movement is a brisk, dashing Scherzo which reminds one of many of Shostakovich's pages, in particular of the Scherzo of the piano quintet. The melody is based on the intervals of the major triad; the accompaniment either stresses the beat with strongly accentuated chords, or supports the uninterrupted rhythmic pulsation. Harsh dissonances which occasionally cut into the diatonic harmony of the Scherzo give it a special dynamism and acuity of sound. The Scherzo is fascinating in its sparkling wittiness. This fantastic outburst is fully justified dramaturgically: without this original *intermezzo* the following (slow) movement would be lacking in conviction.

If the first movement of the Trio can be called an elegy, the third is an epitaph—a short but extremely expressive passacaglia in miniature. Against the background of choral chords of the piano there unfolds a dialog between the violin and violoncello, full of lofty majesty. An unexpected chromatic shift introduces the most important part of the entire work—the Finale.

It begins with an angular, menacing theme. This is replaced by a melody which is similar in character, but sounds even stranger; it is intonated by the piano and accompanied by harsh chords of the violin and violoncello. The mechanical rhythms, the superimposing of automatically repeated middle voices, the gradual growth of sonority—all this creates a monstrously incongruous image. The plaintive intonations of a new theme weave themselves into the automatic motion. The climax is attained: it seems that the infuriated elements are about to consume everything living.

142

But suddenly an invisible curtain is torn asunder. Out of the tumbling cascades of piano figurations swims the theme of the first movement. It sounds excited and passionate, forcing the terrifying vision to retreat. But the latter returns once more, sounding as a menace in the deep basses. A last reminder of the main theme of the first movement; then the violin and violoncello bring in (as an awe-inspiring motto) a fragment from the first theme of the Finale, and the piano chords of the passacaglia terminate the development of the ideas.

The Finale of the Trio is closely related in spirit to the Allegro non troppo from the first movement of the Eighth Symphony.

It has already been stated that the Trio is dedicated to the memory of the composer's friend. Its contents, however, are wider and more objective than the mere expression of feeling caused by the loss of an intimate: they are the outcome of the acute feeling caused by the cruel realities of life. Hence the depth and the high humanism of Shostakovich's Piano Trio, which together with his Seventh and Eighth Symphonies remain truthful, artistic documents of the Great Patriotic War.

The Second Quartet is the direct opposite of the Trio. It is full of light and space. It is a romantic poem, that discloses new angles of the composer's talent. The Quartet consists of four movements: overture, recitative and romance, waltz and variations. The tonal plan of the quartet is worthy of note: A-B-E-A. The melodic richness of its poetic content places it amongst Shostakovich's best works.

The Quartet begins with a swinging, resilient theme which is diatonic with numerous wide intervals, plagal cadences and the characteristic intonations of pan-pipe *cantabiles.* Further on there is a particularly impressive G-major episode, in which the crystal clear cantilena in the high register of the violin sounds against the background of a *pizzicato* on all the other instruments. Towards the end of the Overture a radiant A-major asserts itself. The unexpectedly free course of the melody comes to an end, and the Overture concludes in excitedly happy tones.

The Recitative and Romance carry the listener into the sphere of lyric contemplation. The classicists of the eighteenth century attained perfection in this. It is sufficient to recall the "talking recitatives" of Johann Sebastian Bach. In more recent times Sergei Taneyev was a great master of the recitative. Shostakovich's recitative converts the traditions of Bach and Taneyev to a modern style.

Shostakovich's mastery of melodic development has often been referred to. Yet it has to be mentioned once again, in connection with the recitative and romance of the Quartet. Here it is not only the expressive power of the intonations that is remarkable, but also the unhindered growth of the melody. The unhurriedly unfolding narrative of the violin is distinguished by the breadth of its current and a natural interweaving of melodic intonations. The recitative is full of grave and interrogative intonations.

The romance is of quite a different character. It is simpler in melodic structure and in musical character. It is the calm song of the violin, only interrupted for a short period by an *appassionato* episode. The recitative and romance are a lyric poem for the violin (the rest of the instruments losing their subordinated role). The force of this music lies in the uninterruptedness of the melodic current, its slow tempo, the crystal purity of its lyrical emotion.

144

The Waltz is written in the Russian tradition, its delicate melody is kindred to that of Glinka's famous "Waltz-Phantasia" and to the numerous waltzes of Tchaikovsky. Shostakovich bends this tradition to conform to his own style, and writes a new original page in Russian dance music.

The treatment of the Waltz is noble, simple and limpid; the clarity of the accompaniment contributes to the distinct enunciation of the main theme. This melody, which is first brought in by the violoncello, is full of warmth and romantic dreaminess. The music of the Waltz seems to be woven of cobwebs—so fine are the polyphonic designs, so dainty the melodic outlines, so light the fluttering rhythms. The open-work structure of the Waltz is underlined by the unexpected angularity of the central episode. Shostakovich is a past master at such grotesque juxtapositions. Here the contrast is daring and unexpected; by transferring attention to a new plane of perception, it forces the listener to feel the charm of the main theme of the Waltz with renewed vigor.

The tonality of the Waltz is far remote from that of the Finale (E flat).

To attenuate the sharpness of the transition, Shostakovich connects the two last movements of the Quartet by a short recitative, epically wide and unhurried, which modulates smoothly in the tonality of the Finale. After this appears the variations theme of the Finale.

As in the variations of the First Quartet, the theme is entrusted to an alto solo. Shostakovich always gives considerable attention to the alto in his instrumental chamber *ensembles*, and in both of the Quartets and the Quintet it is entrusted with many significant episodes. The theme

145

contains a multitude of expressions that can be developed as variations; lyrical cantilena is combined with steady progression, and the dominating diatonics with unexpected chromatic turns.

The Finale is the most important and complicated movement of the quartet. The richness of the theme is disclosed in a chain of variations, diverse in form, but joined in dramaturgic unity. In the beginning the theme is exposed by each instrument in turn. The composer seems to be enthralled by the singing melody, which he proceeds to drape in a transparent polyphonic tissue. The movement increases, to concentrate in the forceful passages of the first violin which originate from the intonations of the main theme. From here on begin new phases of variations, the climax of which is an episode where the intonations of the theme sound tensely in the high register of the violin against the background of an organ point (again extremely remote from the basic tonality), accompanied by wild strains of the alto. Then comes the melody of the Recitative, which connected the Waltz to the Finale. It is interwoven with the theme of the latter—the principal theme, with the stately utterance of which the whole composition comes to an end. These pages, together with the finale variations of the Second Piano Sonata, can serve as examples of new principles of variation, on account of their expressive power and the masterly manner of their treatment.

Shostakovich's new Trio and Quartet have entered modern art as something original and never to be repeated. The marvelous lyricism of the romance, the severe meditativeness of the recitative, the elegance of the waltz which combines the qualities of a dance and the phantasy of fluttering chiaroscuros, the majestic grief of the largo (the finale of the Trio)—all are images of exceptional clarity and persuasiveness. They are the work of a great master, of a master in the full force of his talent.

One of the particularly interesting points in the development of Shostakovich's creative genius is the succession of ideas that can be observed in works written at close intervals. It often seems as though the composer could not tear himself away from the images that have struck his imagination, and he keeps returning again and again to the same theme, enriching it with new characteristics.

Thus, for instance, the connection between certain pages of the Eighth Symphony and the dialog of the Piano Trio makes itself clearly felt. In the same manner there is a lot in common between the String Quartet and the Ninth Symphony. The Ninth was the first of Shostakovich's works to appear after the war. It was written in August 1945, and that same year was given its first public performance by the Symphonic Orchestra of the Leningrad Philharmonic with Eugene Mravinski conducting. The first public performance abroad was at a concert of the Prague Philharmonic in December 1945, with Raphael Kubelik holding the baton.

The new symphony is totally different from the two preceding ones both in the character of its music and in its scope. There are five movements in it, but its whole execution takes only twenty-two minutes. The form of the narrative is exceedingly laconic; all connecting elements are reduced to a minimum. The composition of the orchestra is most modest, the orchestral treatment is very limpid and transparent. While the Seventh and particularly the Eighth are characterized by a broad, swinging tonal "al fresco" painting, the Ninth is written in the style of cham-

ber music that reminds one of the early classical symphonies. By this we mean, of course, not stylization, but
similarity of treatment of a symphonic style.

The first movement of the Ninth (Allegro in E-flat
major) is penetrated by a single carefree and happy mood.
There are no emotional contrasts in this graceful and
refined music; the traditional sonata form is obtained from
the juxtaposition of themes which are different in melodic
outline, but common in mood. Both the first theme of the
sonata's Allegro—energetic and clearly outlined, and the
second—joking and provocative, express joy and serenity
to the same degree. This music contains so much vivacity
and moral health, so much humor and inexhaustible joy of
living, and is so spontaneously gay and captivating, that it
seems to be entirely woven of sunbeams and smiles.

The melodic material of the first movement of the Symphony has much in common with the intonations of the
classical style: the themes are markedly diatonic and often
constructed on the harmonic tonalities of the major triad.
At the same time, however, they show the daring use of
interval jumps and chromatic shifts that are so typical of
Shostakovich. The skill with which the composer develops
separate intonations and keeps introducing new witty details into the unfolding of musical ideas is truly extraordinary. His phantasy is absolutely inexhaustible. Despite
the apparent simplicity of the themes and the formal construction, he captivates us by the suddenness of melodic
turns, the cleverness of orchestrational details, and a logic
of development which is subordinated to creative intuition
combined with clearly outlined conception. The rational
source of Shostakovich's creative power is strongly apparent here. But it by no means subjugates his creative spon-

taneity, nor does it lead him to the dryness of "pure constructivism." Shostakovich is never a stylist. The elements of classicism are creatively interwoven in his musical thought. His musical language always remains individualistic, the natural form of expressing thoughts which are purely his own. This is particularly characteristic of the Ninth Symphony.

The second movement, the Moderato, is distinguished by a fine and inspired lyricism.

There is something very meditative, delicately elegiac in it that reminds one of the theme of the Seventh Symphony's Scherzo (of which the composer himself stated that in essence it was "very lyrical"). The main theme is one of Shostakovich's happiest creations: in it, poesy and crystal-pure emotions find their expression in formulas of exclusive clarity and simplicity. In this melody there are a whole row of finest intonational details which would seem to disturb the diatonic principle of its construction, but which in reality are extraordinarily organic and give the melody a particular charm and originality. Such pages, more than anything else, are convincing proof of the originality of Shostakovich's talent. To be novel and original with such strictly limited means of expression is the gift of the chosen few. In the first episode, for instance, we only have the basic melodic line of the clarinet and the parsimoniously outlined bass voice of the violoncello with the double-basses in octave.

Two or three traits are sufficient to disclose the character of Shostakovich's writing. The treatment of the Moderato is extremely simple. The composer seems to have renounced not only all the variety of orchestral coloring, but even extensive utilization of the possibilities of the few instruments included in the score of the second movement. Yet he still proves himself to be an admirable master of orchestration. Take the episode in which the main theme sounds on the flute and oboe (three whole octaves apart), stressed by parallel fifths of the clarinets and oboe. This episode overthrows all the academic laws of harmonization and instrumentation, and if we are to believe scholastic rules, should make an anti-aesthetic impression. But in reality its tonalities are enchanting.

The three last movements of the symphony—Presto, Largo, Allegretto—follow each other without interruption. The connection between them is a very strong one: not on account of a common theme, but precisely because of their abrupt contrast, which stresses the contents of each with particular precision. After the sparkling Scherzo (*presto*) comes the inspired and sad intermezzo, followed by the Finale which sounds so captivatingly gay and juvenile, as it takes us back to the emotions of the symphony's first movement. This is not the first time that Shostakovich has used a similar structure. To mention only one example: in the Piano Quintet, the three last movements also follow each other without interruption and also are captivating by the contrast between their scherzo character and their lyricism. In the Eighth too the three last movements succeed each other without interruption. Despite the three totally different musical images, these three works have similar traits of construction. It would seem that in the Piano Quintet Shostakovich discovered a method of terminating a cycle form which was particularly close to his heart; a method which results in a curious tri-part form, endowed not only with constructive form, but also with deep dramatic significance. In all these examples the finale originates from the collision between the opposing third and fourth movements. Of course, the method varies with each case; its essence, however, remains unchanged.

But to return to the Ninth Symphony. Note the fantastic brilliance and spirited rhythm of the *presto*, which may be classified with Shostakovich's best orchestral Scherzos. The whirlwind nature of the main theme, which is first brought in so effectively by the woodwinds, the clarity of the rhythmical *ostinati* of the strings, against the background of which the trumpet solo sounds unexpectedly pathetic, a marvelous transition to the next movement. All of these combine to convey the impression of a sudden flash of lightning.

The Largo is unusually short and schematic in formal construction: it only occupies four short pages of the score. But its importance in dramatic conception is enormous. It is astonishing in its depth of tragedy, which at first may seem out of place in the light and merry music of the symphony. But this is not so. The Largo is the necessary turning point in the development, the solitary peak from which there opens before us that wide perspective so necessary for understanding the inner meaning of the whole work. It is a return to the past which is impossible to forget, even amidst the joys of peaceful life. This minute of concentrated silence is a tribute of love and endless gratitude to those who saved the world and gave humanity back the very possibility of work and happiness. The Soviet artist Shostakovich could not forget these people at this minute of happy festivity. The very presence of the Largo gives the music of the Symphony a special philosophic significance.

The Largo is written in the form of a dialogue. A menacing unison of the trumpet and trombones, with a recitative on the oboe which is extraordinary in depth and sincerity of feeling. We have already heard its voice in the Seventh, where it sang the requiem to the memory of fallen heroes. Here it sounds just as mournful and inspired. The force of this Largo lies in the dramatic contrast of its dialogue and its musical expressiveness. The treatment is simplified to the fullest possible extent. The means which the composer uses are limited to the unison of the trombones and the trumpet, and the tonalities of the oboe solo against the background of a restrained chord on the strings. That is all!

The transition to the Finale is truly masterly. It is exceedingly laconic, but at the same time persuasive. With the last note of the oboe's recitative, the composer, with extraordinary ease and consistency, goes over to the exposition of the Finale's main theme. Modulation is achieved by a simple shift half a second downwards, C-flat to B-flat. And at once the clarity of the E-flat major tonality is established, in which the Finale of the Symphony is written. . . .

The Finale lacks the impetuosity of the first movement. It is more reserved in motion and more severe in rhythmic pattern, but this does not deprive it of brilliance and freshness in its expression of joy. On the contrary, this feeling finds particular forceful expression in the somewhat measured movement, the energy of the principal themes, the brilliance of the orchestra. The Finale is graceful and witty; its details are all thoroughly worked out; the melodic shifts are unexpected and typical of Shostakovich's polyphonic technique.

Of course, the Ninth Symphony does not occupy the same place in Shostakovich's symphonic creations as do the Fifth, Seventh and Eighth. It is far remote from the philosophical significance and depth of those works. But this does not lessen its importance. It serves to give another proof of the composer's versatility, of the variety of his artistic aims, of his ability to create not only symphonic tragedies, but symphonic scherzos as well—scherzos which embody a world of joyful feelings. It proves the composer's inexhaustible optimism and his brilliant sense of humor. And finally it is the embodiment of the composer's dream —which he had formed long ago—to write a symphony full of cheer, that would bring a smile. That is why we attribute a place of honor in the long row of Shostakovich's works to the Ninth Symphony.

There is one more point which cannot be overlooked. The score of the Ninth is an example of chamber orchestration by a great master. After the grandeur of the Seventh and Eighth, it astonishes by the limpidity of its coloring and the inventiveness with which the composer utilizes limited means, obtaining new and daring effects of tonality. The whole orchestral tissue seems to be woven out of polyphonic designs, of extraordinary delicacy and gracefulness. Every voice is full of life, melodically sapid and expressive. This grandeur of polyphony, in general typical of Shostakovich, is also the distinctive mark of the score of the Ninth Symphony, serving as an example of how a lot may be expressed by few words.

CHAPTER IX

STYLE

A͟т ᴀ ꜰɪʀsᴛ ʜᴇᴀʀɪɴɢ of Shostakovich's music one is struck by the remarkable facility of his style. So effortless is his manner of solving the most complex problems of composition that it would seem nothing is impossible to him. Few of his contemporaries can compare with him in this. Such creative ease, moreover, is a sure sign of great talent and consummate skill. Shostakovich has a remarkable flare for technique. Even in his earliest works he displayed a rare ability for developing his material, constructional precision, and a free mastery of the most intricate devices. Very early, he attained a remarkable grasp of form enabling him to pass from one genre to another at will.

First impressions often prove illusory. That which seems natural may actually have been acquired in long years of practice. Shostakovich, however, always worked with extraordinary facility and speed. As is known, his String Quartet was written in a few days and the superb slow movement of his Fifth Symphony came on a wave of inspiration which held him under its spell for two days. Also known is the fact that he sets his orchestration into the score at once, that he conceives of his compositions in all their detail and writes them down with phenomenal speed. There is something Mozartian in his complete mastery of musical material. This creative facility, however, was not without its dangers. There was the temptation to flaunt his brilliance, to display his faculty of mastering any style and any genre. It seems to us that many of the composer's mistakes were rooted here. This, too, was one of the things which prompted him to stray over tortuous paths instead of taking the highroad of classic art. When these errors and temptations had been overcome, his creative faculty attained the wandlike facility of an accomplished master.

There are two elements at war in Shostakovich's music. On the one hand there is his striving for that which is simple, lucid, for clarity of melody (examples are the themes of the Scherzo in his First Symphony, the E-minor Prelude and Intermezzo of his Pianoforte Quintet) and on the other, there is his trend to that which is pretentious, to the uneven stride of intervals and distortion of fundamental scales. The balance of these trends has varied in the different phases of his development, but both have remained typical of his style. Also characteristic is his penchant for the simplest, even most elementary, melodic, rhythmic and harmonic formulae. This is exemplified by the austere diatonic principle of his E-minor Prelude, the exposition of the Fugue in his Quintet, the variations of his String Quartet. He is equally original in the attainment of orchestral effects by the simplest means. How fresh, for example, is the effect of seemingly stereotype methods of orchestration such as the *pizzicato* and *tremolo* of strings in his Fifth and Sixth Symphonies. His ability to handle accepted methods of composition in a new way, it seems to me, is one of the most remarkable things about Shostakovich.

Variety of genres and content is a feature of his later and more mature works and indicates that his talent has not only broadened, but has grown in depth as well. Though endowed with great creative facility, Shostakovich works carefully and unhurriedly. He assimilates his ideas and impressions thoroughly and is never in too great a rush to set them down. In five years he has written only five major works, but each is unique unto itself and does not repeat its predecessor.

The mature style of Shostakovich, evolved phase by phase from its dormant trends, is already observable in his earliest works. It was enriched, of course, by influences of other masters. He did not borrow the traits of others, however, but, assimilating the various influences, developed those elements which were most suited to his individuality. For example his constructive linearism has a connection with the principles of musical thought laid down in his First Symphony and in essence is the crowning development of these principles. The complexity of his harmony resulted from his characteristic modulatory progressions and the linear weave of his growing melodies. The peculiarity of his melody is due to the wide intervals which already made their appearance in his early works.

One often hears that Shostakovich's melodies are indistinct, difficult to remember and, therefore, not at all his forte. Such assertions are obviously due to misunderstanding. Owing to his interest in the linear principle, he could not do otherwise than draw generously from the mainspring of melody. Actually, his music abounds in superb melodies, flexible, charming and poetic. The examples are numerous: There is the Scherzo of his First Symphony, the themes of the first and second movements of his Pianoforte Concerto, his numerous preludes and nearly all of the main themes of his later symphonic works and chamber music.

To what then can one attribute the assertions that his music is unmelodic? For one thing, it may be due to the novelty of his melody to which not all musicians and music lovers are at once receptive. In the main, however, this may be due to the prevailing one-sided conception of melody. Not all of Shostakovich's melodies lend themselves to the voice. Many of them are suitable only for instruments and depend upon the specific qualities and mode of expression of one or another instrument. Such critics of Shostakovich are making the same mistake that was made by the critics of Berlioz who complained of the great master's "poverty of melody." Shostakovich, who does not "orchestrate" his compositions, but at once includes his instrumentation in the score, conceives of each melody as in a specific timbre often at variance with that one-sided criterion of melody evolving from the vocal principle. The composer, naturally, has also written melodies of a purely vocal character, but most of his melodies are orchestral.

Wide intervals (leaps) are characteristic of Shostakovich's melody. The composer strives to lend independent expression to every tone. He knows that there are no repetitions of tone in various octaves and that their identity of denomination is meant merely to facilitate the writing of music. The notes C in the first and second octave serve as various means of expression for him. Broad progression of intervals lend his melodies an especial freedom of motion and a greater canvas for his color.

Definitions of Shostakovich's style usually connect it with the principles of modern constructive linearism. This *alone*, however, cannot explain the unique originality of his music. The melodic structures of the linearists were nearly always of a calculated nature and, therefore, do not bear

157

comparison with the best pages of Shostakovich. His style, moreover, is linked with certain of the classical traditions, particularly with the traditions of the Russian classics. Here, I should like to stress its connection with the melodic currents of Tchaikovsky. This great Russian master indeed made fullest use of the expressive potential of various registers within the framework of a single melody. This was exemplified by the secondary theme in the first movement of his Sixth Symphony and particularly in its final recurrence before the elaboration. He achieved great beauty in broad strides of interval as evidenced by the love theme of "Romeo and Juliet" and the romance "None But the Lonely Heart." He had the faculty of handling his "space" on many planes. The melodic principles of Shostakovich are somewhat related to all this. The principal difference is that Tchaikovsky frequently and gladly used close intervals by steps, whereas this is rarely true of Shostakovich. Nearly always, the current of his melody is interrupted by broad and daring leaps and these, in fact, lend the respective melodies great expressive force.

It is difficult to speak of Shostakovich's harmony as of something permanent and unchangeable, since it is something that has grown phase by phase through a long process of evolution. There is a striking difference between the harmonic eloquence of his Fifth Symphony and Octet for example, between his Pianoforte Sonata and Pianoforte Quintet. Regardless of this, one may observe certain traits that are common to all.

Shostakovich's harmony frequently seems subordinated to his linear principle, but this does not detract from its value. The composer has merely reverted to the classical conception of harmony as a dynamic factor. The impressionists' delight in "rich pastries" of sound is alien to him. His harmony invariably serves as a powerful means of expression. In his more mature works it is strictly tonal, rarely ventures beyond its framework of major or minor and shuns the complex and ambiguous modes. At times he resorts to the most primitive means of harmonic expression (the elementary juxtaposition of triads). Nevertheless, he is also drawn to unusual progressions of tone, unexpected leaps of modulation and this lends his harmony particular freshness and originality (exemplified by the secondary theme of his Fifth Symphony). Shostakovich does not shrink from dissonance. Applied with great skill in his mature works, it never obscures the main tonal perspective.

Exceptions to this were his polytonal passages which at times led to complete confusion (as in certain bits of his Second Symphony), or at other times were highly effective (as in many parts of "Lady Macbeth of Mtsensk").

Simplicity rather than complexity, however, is characteristic of Shostakovich's more mature works. The composer at times achieves a startling effect literally with a single third. At other times he attains the same results with a long phrase of melody in a single key. Quite often he makes contrasts of strictly diatonic harmonies. Shostakovich's harmony undoubtedly deserves detailed study for its own merits.

The same is true of his composition forms. Most remarkable are their organic integrity, classical proportion and balance. The form of his composition, however, never intrudes itself upon his work as a diagram. He does not compose according to time-honored canons, but weaves live and vivid musical patterns. He has expressed himself in a variety of forms—from the fugue to the sonata, from the simple song to the complex cycle form. Particularly interesting are his sonata forms. In each of these he solves his problems in a different way. Noteworthy is the fact that in his First Symphony he found an interesting way of solving the problem of his recapitulation. In his sonatas the recapitulation is nearly always of a dynamic nature and evolves as something essential because of that which went before rather than as a repetition of it in accordance with the scholastic principle. Shostakovich has a way of briefly summarizing his musical train of thought. His final measures conclude his musical phrases as obviously as a sentence is concluded with a period. This ability to round out his ideas, to construct his composition forms rationally, is probably the composer's chief merit.

Interesting are the composer's principles of linking the component parts of his cyclical forms. Shostakovich achieves this by various means, among them the usual method of establishing kinship between the themes of the various movements. Frequently he builds up his cyclical form on contrasted episodes, but preserves a certain symmetry, returns to his introductory content and, most important, develops it consistently and continuously. Both principles are combined in the construction of his Fifth Symphony and Pianoforte Quintet.

Shostakovich frequently and gladly resorts to the polyphonic forms, among them the fugue, in which he has attained high skill. A single example will do—the Fugue of his Pianoforte Quintet wherein Bach's polyphonic principles are so boldly resurrected. The fugue requires exceptional discipline of musical thought and in the hands of some composers becomes nothing more than an amusing rebus, a mathematical puzzle. There are few who can avail themselves of the fugue for the expression of musical thought, but one of these masters is Shostakovich. Listening to his fugues one is aware not of the cunning counterpoint and highly artificial devices but of their eloquent charm and expressiveness. Though their connection with the classical principles is obvious, one is surprised by their novel application.

Mention of the composer's genres and particularly his use of the so-called popular idioms is in place. The latter, as is known, were extensively used by the Russian classicists. Tchaikovsky indeed was the greatest master in the use of the popular genres. In his hands they were shorn of all that was trivial, served to express the most profound ideas and, simultaneously, were a mighty means of rendering his music accessible to the masses.

Shostakovich no less frequently avails himself of these idioms, but in his hands they acquire another meaning. Tchaikovsky touched upon that vitality of the popular genre which was indiscernible owing to its elementary simplicity, unfolded and carried it to the heights of his art. To Shostakovich, on the other hand, the popular genre is generally an object for parody. As though with a magnifying glass, he reveals its negative principle and regards it as an expression of all that is philistine and smug.

Parody and mockery of the popular genre, however, is often combined with an esthetic admiration for it. At such times he is obsessed with a sense of the grotesque and instead of utilizing the valuable elements of popular music he merely mocks at its limitations.

This is only one side of the question however. Shostakovich's art is manifold and he has availed himself of the popular genre in various ways. As previously mentioned, he availed himself of the waltz genre in the second movement of his concerto and in his G-minor Prelude. Many similar examples may be found in his more mature compositions.

Worthy of mention too is the composer's use of the genre for the purpose of generalization, an important function of the genre in symphonic and opera music. Many interesting examples of this may be found in Shostakovich's music. In "Lady Macbeth" this is exemplified by the pretended lamentation of Catherine, her sentimental romanza and the poignant prisoners' song. More examples may be found in his symphonic music. Shostakovich in his very first symphony made excellent use of the march, waltz and popular ditty. The most striking example of generalization by means of genre is the grisly march in the first movement of his Seventh Symphony. Using the standard means of the military march, the composer effectually depicts the fearful visage of the fascist barbarian. Here there is a happy combination of clarity (owing to the familiar features of the popular genre applied) and philosophical discourse. Here too there is truthful interpretation of psychology and bitterest indignation.

The content of Shostakovich's music is most frequently revealed by the genres he chooses. This does not apply to popular genres alone. Historical genres of classical music are treated by Shostakovich in a new and original manner. To this one should add that he often resorts to the genres of the classical period and rarely to those characteristic of European Romanticism.

Shostakovich has often been termed a neoclassicist. This term has rarely been defined in relation to music and yet it has been applied to such varied composers as César Franck and Brahms, Taneyev and Glazounov. It has also been leveled at many modern composers—Poulenc, Hindemith and others. It is worth while determining, therefore, just what is meant by the neoclassicism of Shostakovich.

One of the main slogans of the neoclassicists was: "Back to Bach!" This was variously understood, and to a considerable extent determined the esthetic position adopted by one artist or another. In the case of such modern linearist-neoclassicists as Paul Hindemith, the question resolved itself through resurrection of the formal principles of Bach which were to be accepted as of self-sufficient esthetic value. The emotional impulses of Bach received secondary consideration. The most important feature of Bach's music, however, was its ideal synthesis of construction and emotional content. Many musical paths and byways of Bach's music led directly to the later classical and romantic principles. All this has been lost from view by the modern linearists, whose conception of Bach is one-sided. Their neoclassicism has nothing in common with the grand spirit of classic art and their esthetic canons when put to practice invariably lead to the bedlam of formalism and emotionless constructivism.

For neoclassicists like Taneyev or Brahms the turn towards Bach (as also towards Mozart, Palestrina and Orlando di Lasso) was quite different. With them it was a sort of reaction against the excesses of romanticism (Brahms) or against the luxuriant arts of the modernists (Taneyev).[1] In the works of the great masters of the past they sought for those waters of life which should render fruitful the barren soil (as it seemed to them) of modern art. For this reason they did not so much strive to resurrect

[1] The music of Bach had a special attraction for César Franck owing to various religious associations which conformed to his world outlook.

the constructive principles of Bach (though the latter were of enormous importance in the formation of their own respective styles) as to seek inspiration from the moral and esthetic principle of classical music, opposing austerity and purity of musical thought to the sensuality and high coloring of the Romanticists. They aimed to resurrect that which was most valuable in classical music, its spirit and not its letter.

The neoclassicism of Shostakovich is closer to that of Taneyev than to that of the modern Western composers (though he to a certain extent evolved the creative principles of the latter). In his mature works the neoclassicist principle is revealed not in the resurrection of the conventional, constructive methods of the old masters, but rather in an approach to their method of thought, and a return to the austerity of esthetic principles. As distinct from many of his contemporaries Shostakovich has revived the great humanistic traditions of classicism on a new basis, has created an art highly intellectual and yet permeated with human emotion. It is in this that he has drawn near to the neoclassicism of Taneyev. His outlook, however, differs from that of this splendid Russian composer and theoretician. Neoclassicism to Shostakovich did not imply surmounting and breaking with the heritage of Romanticism and modernism (as it did to Taneyev). Certain features of Shostakovich's artistic individuality drew him close to the principles of the old masters. He was attracted by their profound meditation and stately grandeur—the music of Bach and Handel. He was drawn to the linear method of expression which sprang from Bach. He was also drawn to their composition forms (particularly the polyphonic), their style of instrumentation (wherein the melodic principle predominated) and to their technique of frequently using passages (scale sections).

Shostakovich has often been accused of eclecticism. Much has been made of the varied phenomena appearing in his music. Actually, however, Shostakovich, like any other composer, could not help but undergo a period in which he assimilated those styles which were nearest to him. This process may develop in different ways and its results too may be varied. One composer might stop half way and for all time preserve the traces of unassimilated influences—the cause of his eclecticism. Another might pass through manifold influences, choose the methods most suitable to himself and weld them into a style of his own. It is this which accounts for the originality and the spirit of innovation of the great artists. Shostakovich, undoubtedly, belongs to the latter group. The phenomena which attracted his attention were numerous and his susceptibilities acute. Owing to his extraordinary talent, he quickly assimilated the various styles and genres. This process sometimes developed so swiftly, tempestuously, that the composer did not always get a firm grip on the new elements and in such cases, of course, his music did display something of eclecticism. Examples of this are his Pianoforte Sonata and his ballets "Golden Age" and "Bolt." Very soon, however, he evolved a new style in which all previous influences had been transformed beyond recognition and merged into something that was monolithic and original.

The wide range of influences which move a composer attest not to the poverty but to the richness of his intellect, if he is able to suit them to his needs. This is perfectly true of Shostakovich's music and attests to its sound ties with world musical culture.

As for the contradictions of his melodic and harmonic principles, of which so much has been said, these too do not attest to omnivorous eclecticism, but to the fact that the composer was painstaking in his choice of means wherewith to express one idea or another in music. His style is indeed unique for its assimilation of so many different artistic devices.

Shostakovich's creative methods have changed at various periods. At a certain time he was much swayed by the alogical principle, which clashed with the logical cast of thought mainly characteristic of him. The alogical features are revealed by the leaps in his progression which, as it were, sever the thread of his harmony. They are once more revealed in melodic phrases deliberately deprived of continuity. The alogical principle, however, was not something native to Shostakovich, but evolved when he developed the intellectual creative method to its extreme. This deserves attention.

The intellectual and emotional elements are frequently posed one against the other in art. There are artists whose work is dominated by the rational and constructive principle, by cool calculation proscribing spontaneous expression. In the case of others, Scriabin for example, the rational principle serves as a guard against diffuse improvisation and lends the current of his emotions both form and purpose. Still others are so firmly in the grip of their lyrical emotion that their work often suffers from defects in construction. Listed here are the main tendencies, but this does not exclude the possibility of merging the rational with the emotional. Absolute rationalization is unthinkable in art. Abstract rhetoric is alien to art and wherever it predominates one might say something about skill and the

166

ability to deal with material, be it marble, the written word or music, but not about art which would be impossible and useless if excluded from artistic imagery influencing human perception.

Philosophical and emotional currents are invariably combined in the best works of art ("Faust," for example). This, too, is true of music. The apostles of musical intellectualism generally argue that the specific nature of music, allegedly divorced from meaning, offers wide possibilities for abstract "argumentation." Seeking for an example, they frequently refer to Bach whose music, they believe, is purely of the kingdom of the intellect. Actually, however, Bach's music is based on very real emotion and not at all on immanent logic of unemotional sound construction. Like all great masters he was deeply moved by the musical ideas which inspired his compositions. Intellectualism in music therefore must be regarded as a train of logic guarding against the capricious ebb and flow of emotions and not at all as a rejection of the emotional for the sake of abstract, mathematical computation.

Such intellectualism may be found in Shostakovich's art, particularly of the later period. His works bear the traces of intense searching and penetrating thought. His symphonies, for example, happily combine the philosophical with the emotional (as evidenced by the Fifth and Seventh). The term, intellectualism, as applied to the music of Shostakovich, therefore must be understood as breadth of vision which enables him to encompass the emotional and the philosophical elements, to achieve a synthesis of two contradictory principles by sheer will and unceasing creative thought.

Shostakovich achieved this quality after surmounting

167

many dangers. The first was his deviation into alogical tendencies and dry constructivism. The second and perhaps most serious was his deviation into naturalism. Shostakovich possesses the sharp perceptive faculties of an artist. No details can escape him. He also possesses a rare gift for description and can capture the characteristic features of his model very adroitly in his music. Far from detrimental, these are the strong sides of his talent. Under the influence of certain esthetic principles, however, these tendencies led him to naturalism, which had such a sad effect on his operas "The Nose" and "Lady Macbeth."

The term grotesque is frequently applied to Shostakovich's music. It is generally attributed to the influences of the 1920's, when a certain sort of grotesquerie was prevalent in art. To understand the grotesqueries of Shostakovich, however, one should approach the matter from several angles and with historical perspective and not rest content with a definition of grotesquerie as applicable to modern masters.

The grotesque, as is known, had its origin in ancient times. There is no need to delve into the too hoary past. The grotesqueries of Swift and Rabelais are sufficient. A master of the grotesque principle was Hoffman. Outstanding Russian masters of this principle were Gogol, Dostoyevsky and Shchedrin. Grotesquerie in our days is observable in the works of many artists of various tendencies. It is necessary to distinguish therefore between the different conceptions of this element entertained by various authors. There were some who used it as a potent means of satire (Swift and Shchedrin). Others applied it for its own sake, adopted it as a style and nothing more. The historic content of grotesque art, moreover, has often been distorted by subsequent generations of artists. An example is the tragic grotesquerie of Goya which served as a most powerful means of human protest against the cruelty of war and national enslavement, a means by which the artist so effectively scourged brutishness, hypocrisy and superstition. And yet it was interpreted by the more modern, expressionistic artists as a poesy of nightmares and pathological horrors. Something similar may be observed in the sphere of music. Comparison of the grotesquerie of Berlioz (Finale of his "Fantastic Symphony"), of Liszt (Mephistopheles in the symphony "Faust"), of Mahler, of Tchaikovsky ("Nutcracker Suite"), of Alban Berg's "Wozzeck" or Stravinsky's "Moor" will suffice to make us realize what a wide difference of conceptions exist concerning one and the same artistic principle.

Shostakovich applied the grotesque principle in various ways. In a number of his works it assumed the shape of exaggeration, of caricaturing realities (his operas and ballets). This is akin to the traditions of Western European art in the 1920's. Shostakovich learned to handle such grotesquerie with consummate skill and by exceptionally brilliant virtuosity achieved a series of brief and witty satirical sketches. This virtuosity however, harbored the danger of transition to the petty musical anecdote which might indeed supersede the virile satire of the great masters of the grotesque. As his gifts developed and his radius of artistic vision grew, he quite naturally drifted from the primitive application of such grotesque principles. The grotesquerie of his later works is infinitely more significant.

In his mature works Shostakovich does not avail himself of the grotesque principle merely for the purpose of emphatic caricature. More varied here, the grotesque principle is allied to the classical and at times to romantic esthetics. Here too an important role devolves on dual principles of construction, on the contrast of the tragic and the comic, on offsetting one with the other unexpectedly, on the surprise of a tragic finish to a comic episode. In this he drew near to the symphonic method of Tchaikovsky who masterfully availed himself of a dual construction and grotesque juxtapositions of contrary moods (the Scherzo in the Finale of his Sixth Symphony for example). It is probable, too, that Mahler derived this principle from Tchaikovsky (the influence of Tchaikovsky on Mahler has not been properly appraised to the present day).

The tendency to philosophize over realities predominates in the later works of Shostakovich. This explains his penchant for certain genres—particularly the genre of the symphony set forth as a philosophical tragedy (his Fifth and Seventh Symphonies). This too accounts for the intellectualism of his music. Few works of modern art can equal the profundity of these symphonies and Pianoforte Quintet. Thought and feeling, philosophical detachment and fervent emotion are harmoniously blended here. Shostakovich's mature works differ from his early compositions precisely in that his brilliant, though often superficial reception and reflection of realities have been superseded by earnest and significant musical discourses touching upon the most important phases of Soviet life (the birth of a new social and individual consciousness, the Patriotic War and heroism of the Soviet people). The philosophical import of Shostakovich's music is great and who can tell but that it may one day acquaint our descendants with the spirit of our times more convincingly than dozens of ponderous volumes.

Rich and varied is the composer's world of artistic

imagery. Whereas one could formerly observe a certain one-sidedness in his work unduly stressing the grotesque tangents and angular caricature, his more mature works are remarkable for their variety of emotion ranging from tragic pathos to sparkling witticism, from powerful assertion of the force of life to tender lyricism. This is due to the rich spiritual world of the composer. The predominating tendency of the mature Shostakovich is to release the higher human impulses, against puppetry and automaton-like grotesquerie in order to create a broader art, of vital and philosophical meaning. The humanist quality of Shostakovich's music impressed itself upon the listener with particular force especially at the time when all the world so anxiously followed the struggle of progressive mankind against the dark forces of barbarism and brutishness. We are proud of Shostakovich's works because they reflect so effectually the sentiments and ideas of the new man.

The skill, original style and rich content of his works draw Shostakovich near to the great classics. He has indeed approached the heights of classic art perhaps more closely than any of his contemporaries.

No less important than an esthetic appraisal of Shostakovich's music is an elucidation of its genesis and the composer's relation to modern Western European and Soviet art. A talent such as his could not help but assimilate many varied trends of art. It is far from easy to define them in his work, however, since they have been transformed by his individuality.

First consideration should be given to the relation and ties existing between his music and that of the Russian classics. Superficial and one-sided criticism has often denied his music the traits of nationalism and therefore proclaimed him a "Westerner." A number of foreign critics on the other hand have stressed the Slavic character of his music and indicated numerous traits which it shares with the Russian music of the nineteenth century. Shostakovich's art, of course, is truly Russian, though in his music the national principle assumes a form quite different from that in the works of other composers. This again attests to the composer's extraordinary gifts. The great Goethe believed that "the most exalted and difficult thing in art is an understanding of that which is individual." Shostakovich is well endowed with this faculty.

He was reared in the spirit of the so-called Petersburg school. Maximilian Steinberg, who propagated the creative principles of Rimsky-Korsakov, and Alexander Glazounov, the last of the Mohicans of the "new Russian school," played an important role in the formation of the young composer's individuality (this was evidenced by many details in the orchestration of his First Symphony and also in his later works). Many years thereafter, Shostakovich wrote about the importance of Rimsky-Korsakov's skill of orchestration which, he was convinced, had exercised strong influence on the whole of modern music. "Rimsky-Korsakov and his pupil and continuator (in the principles of instrumentation) I. Stravinsky," he wrote, "were the teachers of orchestration for an entire generation of composers. Personally, I have no doubt as to the exceptional significance of Tchaikovsky's scores to all modern orchestration. . . . Any opera, any symphony of Tchaikovsky may serve as an example of how a symphony orchestra should be used. Rimsky-Korsakov and Tchaikovsky brought the traditions of the great Glinka to Russian and world music. Glinka's discourse on orchestration, covering no more than a few

172

pages, is probably the most profound and subtle exposition ever written on the art of orchestration. The role of Russian musicians in the history of the post-Beethoven symphony, of course, was not limited to achievements in the sphere of technique alone. The symphony epoch launched by Beethoven produced such outstanding musicians as Berlioz, Liszt, Wagner and Mahler, but the honor of being the true continuer of Beethoven fell to the Russian composer Tchaikovsky. To the profundity of the Beethoven symphony Tchaikovsky added that passionate lyrical emotion and clear expression of intimate human feeling which rendered the symphony—the most complex genre of musical art—accessible and dear to the masses." [2]

These words indicate a perfect understanding of the great Russian masters.

There are firm ties between the music of Shostakovich and that of such fledglings of the Petersburg school as Igor Stravinsky and Serge Prokofieff. Even such early works of Shostakovich as his "Fantastic Dances," the First Symphony and, to a certain extent, the Pianoforte Sonata, were akin in spirit to Prokofieff in their tendency to negate the modern trends of art. In his later works too these ties are felt in the elasticity of rhythm and in certain features of his harmony (the peculiar use of elementary thirds). Shostakovich's indebtedness to Stravinsky has manifold aspects which can be traced in the influence of that composer's work, from "The Wedding" to the "Little Suite," from "Punchinello" to "Symphony of Psalms," from "Petrushka" to "Oedipus Rex." Here, however, Shostakovich was influenced mainly by Stravinsky's skill of orchestration. He did not copy its

[2] D. Shostakovich, "Great Culture of the Slavs." From the newspaper "Literature and Art," April 15, 1942.

details of course. Such a method of assimilation belongs only to the mediocre. The true artist independently applies the main principles of his predecessors. His study of Stravinsky's scores unfettered Shostakovich's train of musical thought from many dogmas of scholasticism. It is in this and not in certain similarities of method (unquestionable in places) that the influence of the author of "Petrushka" and "Rite of Spring" is to be found. Here, too, Shostakovich derived much of his acumen for the unusual solution of problems when dealing even with simple and elementary material. Shostakovich's grotesqueries are also rooted here (Stravinsky's "Little Suite" is indeed an encyclopedia of modern musical grotesquerie). This, oddly enough, brings us once more to the most important mainspring of Shostakovich's art, to the great Tchaikovsky who exercised such strong influence on so many composers.

The grotesquerie of Tchaikovsky, expressed in many of his works, from the artless "March of the Tin Soldiers" to the fearful vision of the "Queen of Spades," from the "Nutcracker Suite" to the Scherzo in his Sixth Symphony, could indeed teach Shostakovich very much. The relationships between certain passages of the First Symphony and the grotesque music of "Nutcracker Suite" have already been mentioned. This affinity is even more striking in the war theme of Shostakovich's Seventh. Availing himself of the abrupt grotesquerie peculiar to the Scherzo of Tchaikovsky's Sixth Symphony, Shostakovich effectually depicted the brutish and obtuse cruelty of the foe. Igor Glebov,[3] one of the best connoisseurs of Tchaikovsky's music, interpreted the Scherzo of the "Pathetique" Symphony as a "flow of evil forces," as the triumph of misanthropy. A similar inter-

[3] Nom de plume of Boris Assafyev.

pretation could be given to the war theme of Shostakovich's Seventh Symphony. There is much that is similar in the construction of these two compositions. Both at first seem essentially harmless, curious and puzzling. But then they grow into something that is ominous, heavy, implacable. There is an increment of noise, outcries and savagery. These are independent phenomena of style, however; as independent, in fact, as the inimitable creative individuality of each of these composers.

Tchaikovsky's influence was not limited to the sphere of grotesquerie alone. The dramatic ardor of his symphonic music also influenced the best pages of Shostakovich's polyphony. The theme of the Fifth Symphony, its psychological profundity and motive of struggle to free mankind from the yoke of prejudice is also closely related to Tchaikovsky's symphonic music. Shostakovich successfully combined the philosophical with the "passionate, lyrical emotion and clearest expression of intimate human feeling which rendered the symphony—the most complex genre of musical art—accessible and dear to the masses." Shostakovich, perhaps, more convincingly and vividly than any other composer in our days developed the *general* principles of the Tchaikovsky symphony, so remote from him in character, but related to him in purport.

There are other ties too between the music of Shostakovich and that of the Russian classics. Certain features of Mussorgsky's harmony, skill and eloquence of expression are not foreign to him. The same is true of Glinka's austerely spare principles of art, his brevity and fondness for transparent orchestration.

Shostakovich's music owes yet another of its features to the influence of Glinka—its linear train of thought. His penchant for continuous development of melody and poly-phonic evolution owes its origin to the classical traditions (particularly of Bach) as well as to the influences of Western modern music. This is only natural. But one should not forget that linearism too has long been associated with certain features of Russian music. Here again one must refer to the great Glinka whose polyphonic skill in the construc-tion of secondary patterns is common knowledge. This is sufficiently evidenced by the score of "Kamarinskaya." There is more truth than is generally supposed in Tchai-kovsky's words: "The whole of the Russian symphonic school is enclosed in 'Kamarinskaya' like the oak in its acorn." There were many offshoots from this remarkable work which told on the art of Stravinsky and influenced the linear character of Shostakovich's music. One must also remember that Shostakovich too is a fledgling of the Peters-burg school, that from early youth he associated with Glazounov, great master of Russian polyphony. Another master who is near to Shostakovich is Sergei Ivanovich Taneyev, one of the most important representatives of the Moscow school and distinguished for his constructive logic, skill of polyphony and undeniable neoclassicism. The similarity here consists in the principles of melody construc-tion (this was mentioned by V. Protopopov in his article "Musical Language of Taneyev" published in the magazine "Soviet Music" in 1940). Shostakovich himself has said that he studied and knows very well the chamber music of Taneyev.[4]

[4] A few words are in place about this remarkable Russian musician who, unfortunately, is not sufficiently well known beyond the confines of his country. The favorite pupil of Tchaikovsky, Taneyev succeeded him as the teacher of the theory classes in the Moscow Conservatory. Taneyev was a man of superior intellect, iron will and discipline. His activities were greatly varied. He was a brilliant composer and pianist

Shostakovich's linearism, finally, may be associated with the involved features of the Russian folk song, its rich and original subvoices. This mainspring of music also served the needs of Glinka, Taneyev and other masters of Russian counterpoint.

Another side of the national character of Shostakovich's music is its affinity to Russian folk melody. At a first glance it would seem that his music, perhaps with the exception of the fourth act of "Lady Macbeth of Mtsensk," is barren of local color. The close relationship between his melody and Russian folk melody, however, is evidenced by such sonorous themes as those of the E-minor Prelude, of the Quartet variations and the Fugue of his Pianoforte Quintet. His method of applying the folk melody is most individual. He does not strive for that which is ethnographic. Though he, too, drew upon the elements of folk music, these were interwoven with many others in his consciousness. His method of assimilating the folk melody is somewhat akin to that of Tchaikovsky. Another thing in which he resembles this master is his use of the urban popular song, his interest in the "music of everyday life" which was rejected by the worshippers of the "Big Five" (Catherine's romanza "Through the Window Recently I Saw" is but one example). Shostakovich also revealed deep understanding of the old peasant song, as evidenced by the choruses in the fourth act of "Lady Macbeth of Mtsensk." Despite its cosmopolitan character, Shostakovich's music is bound firmly with the Russian national traditions.

(a pupil of Nikolai Rubinstein), a profound student of music and one of its outstanding authorities (the author of the monumental works on research of theory: "Active Counterpoint of Old Music" and "Study of the Canon") and a teacher. Several generations of Russian musicians owe their musical education to Taneyev.

The national character of his music, moreover, is revealed by the content of his best works. The profound psychology, ethical message and moving sincerity of his Fifth and Seventh Symphonies and Pianoforte Quintet would be unthinkable without his close ties with the art of the great Russian masters of the last century. These traditions, of course, are presented in a new way. Shostakovich is not merely a Russian composer, but a composer of modern Russia and, most important, a Soviet artist. The content and spirit of his works, inspired by Soviet realities, express the thoughts and sentiments of the Soviet man and woman (best shown by the Seventh Symphony). It is in this (and not only in his ties with the Russian classics) that the national essence of his music is to be found. He has indeed continued the classic traditions, but under new, Soviet conditions. It was proximity to his native soil which enabled him to create a work of great moral, ethical and social importance.

His ties with Russian music, of course, did not exclude the Western influences which played so important a role in the creative development of Shostakovich. Nor is he the only Russian composer who found his style in a synthesis of the national traditions and the best traditions of Western European art. This was also true of Glinka.

Unlike most Russian composers who were drawn to the romantic music of the nineteenth century, Shostakovich was attracted by the classic and pre-classic masters. This is revealed by his choice of genre, his conception of the cyclical form of chamber music, his style of instrumentation and certain pages of his works pervaded with austere grandeur (the Largo of his Fifth Symphony, the Prelude and Fugue of the Pianoforte Quintet) and, finally, by the superb balance of his forms and laconic exposition. In Shostakovich's music, however, the old traditions are revived in a modern manner and are enriched by the influences of the Russian classics. Similarly assimilated by the composer were certain phenomena of modern Western European art. The influences of the latter were most pronounced and not limited, as is generally supposed, to the sphere of music alone.

Among the masters of the post-classical era it was Gustav Mahler who exercised considerable influence upon Shostakovich. There was special reason for this. The Leningrad musicians in the late 1920's studied Mahler with special eagerness, and Shostakovich was no exception. In Mahler's music, in fact, he found something that was native to him: the human tendency of the Mahler symphony, its penetrating psychology, virile irony and the poignant tragedy of its conflicts, qualities which attest to a complete command of the modern symphonic orchestra and daring innovation of orchestration. Shostakovich learned much from the author of "Song of the Earth" and "Symphony of a Thousand." Drawn as he was to the grand canvas of the symphony, he most naturally turned to Mahler.

Though the Mahler influences were pronounced, this factor should not be overstressed. These influences formed but *one* element which contributed to the formation of Shostakovich's style. One should remember that much which at first glance seems to have come from Mahler, was actually prompted by Tchaikovsky.

The influence exerted upon Shostakovich by such Western composers as Hindemith, Alban Berg and others has already been mentioned. These, however, proved to be

179

of a passing nature and were largely surmounted by the composer in his more mature works. More important was the effect upon his work of other phenomena of modern Western art. The connections of his work with these were by no means few.

What could there be in common, one might ask, between this Russian composer and Charles Chaplin, the great artist of the cinema? And yet there are many points of similarity: humanism, subtle psychology and mastery of the grotesque. I should also like to compare the music of Shostakovich with the later works of Pablo Picasso. This refers to such canvases as "The Destruction of Guernica," in which the artist pilloried the fascist murderers. Most remarkable is the fact that the artist here deals with a theme that is new to him using those means of expression which evolved from his earlier principles.[5] In his own and truly modern language Shostakovich in his Seventh Symphony similarly depicts the heroism of the Soviet people. Both artists are united in their hatred for the fascist and also by the fact that they were able to voice this hatred by a means of expression peculiar to themselves and therefore very convincing. There is an important difference, however, in the course taken by each of these works. Picasso's painting brands the fascist savages and evokes hatred for them. In Shostakovich's Symphony the bestiality of fascism is confronted with the mighty forces of mass heroism which ultimately shattered the invasion of the barbarians.

Shostakovich, too, is near to the spirit of a number of modern writers, whose vital comprehension of realities,

[5] The more fully to express the chaos and horror of destruction, Picasso availed himself of his earlier principles of combining planes, especially in place here.

modern principles of art and hatred for fascist obscurantism are qualities shared by the composer of the Seventh Symphony.

I do not, of course, intend to put a mark of equation between Shostakovich's work and that of the Western artists. The works of our composer contain much that is characteristic of his country alone and are closely bound with modern Soviet life. They are, however, allied to the best and most progressive works of Western European art and since all advanced forces are now united in the common cause of the progressive Democratic ideals it is especially important to note the Russian composer's proximity to the most important phenomena of modern art in the West. Only this will reveal the full significance of Shostakovich's art which has inherited the best traditions of the Russian classics and is so strongly linked with the strivings of the most advanced artists of our times. This too reveals the truly modern character of Shostakovich's music and explains its exceptional popularity throughout the world. The art of this master is indeed profoundly national and intimately connected with the whole of Soviet culture. It is interlaced, nonetheless, with the best and most progressive elements of world art and is, therefore, cosmopolitan and international in nature. The significance and timeliness of their content, their refreshing originality, eloquence of expression and progressive character place the mature works of Shostakovich among the most outstanding creations of world culture. The realization of this is growing with the appearance of each new work of the master.

Some critics are inclined to regard Shostakovich's numerous musical ties as eclecticism. This is decidedly untrue. For one thing, the composer assimilated all influences in his own, most independent way. For another, we find that only a strict choice of influences told upon his music. Not by any means all, but only those which were native to him came within the range of his vision. This attests to the independence of his thinking. Breadth of vision and an eagerness to learn are his most outstanding traits. He strove consistently to enrich his art with all that was valuable and to assimilate the widest possible range of elements. In this respect he resembles Tchaikovsky and Mozart who also assimilated the most varied influences of art.

This comparison with Mozart might seem presumptuous to some, but it is made for a particular reason. There is no attempt, of course, to commensurate the talents of these composers. Such comparisons are nearly always fruitless. We who are contemporaries of Shostakovich would find it difficult to do so with any measure of certainty. The comparison pertains only to the similarity of social and historical functions of the art of Mozart and Shostakovich. Like the author of "Don Juan," the Soviet composer assimilated a wide range of tendencies modern and old. He has, therefore, attained the universal quality of Mozart's art more closely than any other modern composer. And if Mozart achieved a synthesis of the musical tendencies of his times and created an art expressive of the progressive esthetic principles of his epoch, the same is largely true of the music of Shostakovich.

Shostakovich is indeed an artist of his times, one who is bound to modern culture with many ties. A national composer reared in the traditions of the Russian classic school, he founded an art of world-wide importance. His mature works express the most progressive strivings of mankind and it is to this that his music owes its truly modern character.

It is not elementary propaganda by means of one form of art or another that is in question here, but the general progressive trend of art which serves as a mighty weapon for struggle. It is not essential to write about current events to express the advanced ideas of civilization. Only that art is of our times which reflects the grandeur and nobility of human nature, the most exalted strivings of man which the modern barbarians tried so hard to paralyze. The future belongs only to art such as this and not to soulless and ugly formalism.

Some critics abroad have maintained that only music with political content is demanded in the Soviet Union, whereas, actually, there is only good music or bad. Works of art, of course, may be well done or poorly done, may be original to a greater or lesser degree. Aside from this, however, people have always been interested primarily in the message conveyed by the artist, the sentiments and feelings which moved his fantasy. The history of world art has shown that the greatest masters were always inspired by that which was human and progressive and in their works lent expression precisely to these. No art that has been nurtured by barbarism and reaction can be truly great.

The progressive tendencies were always characteristic of the art of the Russian classics and it is this which won them world recognition. The Soviet artists are striving to continue this tradition. We judge a work of art for its accord with the great ideas of our times, since art, to us, represents an important part of culture and not merely a pretty toy. This, naturally, does not exclude purely esthetic appraisal. To us, in fact, the two aspects are indivisible.

Returning to Shostakovich, we find it not at all difficult to perceive the exceptional importance of his art since his works not only shine because of their original style and bril-

183

liant fantasy, but are also permeated with the most progressive ideas of our times. The human quality and truthfulness of his Fifth Symphony, the clarity of expression of his Quartet, philosophic lyricism of his Quintet and heroic spirit of his Seventh Symphony cannot help but move the heart of every honest person and every citizen of our country. Though his music mirrored the Soviet realities, Shostakovich became a truly international artist whose works have endeared him to the entire world. This can readily be explained by the fact that the strivings of Soviet culture are interlaced with those of all progressive mankind. When foreign orchestras play Shostakovich's Seventh Symphony, this symphony born of Russian heroism cannot help but spread those sentiments and feelings which are shared by the whole of the Soviet people.

In Conclusion

The personality of the composer is indivisibly connected with his art. Many admirers of his works would like to know more about him. The following sketch of Shostakovich may do something to satisfy their curiosity.

In one of his recent articles, the writer Eugene Petrov said that Shostakovich resembles a model schoolboy. . . . It is true that there is something very youthful about the composer. Long years of hard work, successes and disappointments have left their stamp upon him, but nothing could efface his youthful spontaneity or extinguish the twinkle of his bespectacled grey eyes.

He is of medium height and thin. His face is pale and a tuft of unruly hair permanently dominates his high forehead. His movements are quick but not hurried, impetuous but not abrupt. He is a good conversationalist, a man of tact, one who can listen carefully, and quickly comprehend what he hears. His speech too is quick, his phrases clear and brief. It is necessary to see Shostakovich with his friends to realize what humor there is in the man, what a home body and good comrade he is.

Simplicity is perhaps his most charming feature. He does not at all belong to those who are hypnotized by their fame and therefore seclude themselves behind inaccessible barriers. Shostakovich's bearing is simple and even a little shy. When thunderous applause draws him onto the stage, he clutches nervously for the hand of the conductor, jerkily takes his bow to the roaring audience and hurries from the hall. This is the awkwardness of a plain and modest man moved and yet taken aback by the affection displayed for him by the people. The private life of the composer is similarly plain and modest. He is not fond of unrestrained praise and is always his own severe, sometimes too severe, critic.

His is a kindly and responsive nature. Every mark of talent in his pupils is a sincere pleasure to him and he lends a ready ear to each student or young musician who comes to him for advice or aid. Musicians are not the only ones who come to him for advice. Holding the office of deputy to the Leningrad City Soviet, he gave careful attention to the requests of his electors and did all he could to satisfy them. In 1942 Shostakovich was the president of the Kuibyshev Union of Soviet Composers and in this capacity labored solicitously to better the conditions of his colleagues.

He has always been the loyal and responsive friend of

the young composers, always listens to their works attentively, is always ready to discuss their compositions, measure by measure, and never hesitates sincerely to express his opinion. He knows how to indicate shortcomings and merits, how to nurture and encourage every spark of talent. For this the younger composers repay him with affection and respect.

He is fond of life in all its aspects and is not inclined to stay within the four walls of his study. He is drawn to the spaces of the stadiums where football matches are furiously in progress on the green. His own football style is spontaneous and temperamental—much like his music. More than an average football fan, he is a great connoisseur of the game and constantly in touch with sporting events. On the wall of his study there is his own chart of the games that were played for the football cup of the U.S.S.R. He can easily cite the names of all football players of importance and discuss the merits of each. He has more than once journeyed all the way from Leningrad to Moscow to attend a particularly interesting game.

The composer's range of interests is wide. He keeps well abreast of the latest books, films and plays. Busy though he is, he finds the time to write articles about the latest operas. He is enamoured of all that is Russian: ". . . I am proud that I am a Russian. I am proud to be the son of a people which brought forth the great Lenin. I am proud to be a Slav and to belong to that people which gave the world such giants as Pushkin and Leo Tolstoi. I am proud that my blood brothers, the Poles, gave world culture such an author as Mickiewicz, that the Serbs, related to me, have produced an epos that has been admired by civilized mankind for centuries.

186

"As a musician I am proud of the fact that the music of my country holds a place of honor in world musical culture. The sons of the Russian people, Glinka, Borodin, Mussorgsky and Tchaikovsky, were great composers all, and their art has lost none of its delight for more than a century. The Slavic people have played an enormous role in the cultural development of mankind. . . ." (From his speech at the Second All-Slav Meeting.)

These words reveal Shostakovich as a Russian, as a man who loves his country dearly, as a tireless searcher in art, a continuer of the traditions of the great masters of Russian music and one who is filled with respect for the art of other nations. These words reveal the personality of a progressive and advanced artist of our times.

WORKS OF DMITRI SHOSTAKOVICH

Op. 1   Scherzo for Orchestra. 1919. Manuscript.
Op. 2   8 Preludes for Pianoforte. 1919–20. Manuscript.
Op. 3   Themes and Variations for Orchestra. 1921–22. Manuscript.
Op. 4   2 Fables by Krylov for Voices and Orchestra ("The Cricket and the Ant," "The Ass and the Nightingale"). 1922. Manuscript.
Op. 5   3 Fantastic Dances. 1922. Music Publishing House, 1926. (Known in U. S. as Op. 1.)
Op. 6   Sonata for Two Pianofortes. 1922. Manuscript.
Op. 7   Scherzo for Orchestra, E-flat Major. 1923. Manuscript.
Op. 8   Trio (Pianoforte, Violin, Violoncello). 1923. Manuscript.
Op. 9   Three Pieces for Violoncello and Pianoforte (Fantasy, Prelude, Scherzo). 1923–24. Manuscript.
Op. 10 First Symphony. 1924–25. Music Publishing House, 1926. Premiere on May 12, 1926, Leningrad Philharmonic, under baton of N. Malko.
Op. 11 Octet (4 Violins, 2 Violas, 2 Violoncellos) (Prelude and Scherzo). 1925. Music Publishing House, 1927.
Op. 12 Sonata for Pianoforte. 1926. Music Publishing House, 1927.
Op. 13 "Aphorisms," 10 Pieces for Pianoforte. "Triton" Publishing House.
Op. 14 Second Symphony ("Dedication to October"). 1927. Music Publishing House, 1927. Premiere on November 6, 1927, Leningrad Philharmonic, under baton of N. Malko.
Op. 15 "The Nose"—Opera in 3 Acts. Libretto by Y. Preis, based on the novel of N. Gogol. 1927–28. Manuscript.

Premiere on January 13, 1930, Leningrad Little Opera House under baton of S. Samosud.

Op. 16   "Tahiti Trot" (Orchestra transcription). 1928. Manuscript.

Op. 17   Two pieces by D. Scarlatti (transcribed for military band). 1928. Manuscript.

Op. 18   Music for the film "New Babylon." 1928–29. Manuscript.

Op. 19   Music for the comedy "The Flea," by V. Mayakevsky. 1929. Manuscript.

Op. 20   Third Symphony ("First of May"). 1931. Music Publishing House, 1932. Premiere on November 6, 1931, Leningrad Philharmonic under baton of A. Gauk.

Op. 21   Six romanzas to the words of Japanese poets for voices and orchestra ("Love," "Before Suicide," "Immodest Glance," "First and Last Time," "Love," "Death"). 1928–31. Manuscript.

Op. 22   "Golden Age"—ballet in 3 acts (suite from music of ballet published by Music Publishing House, 1934). 1929–30. Manuscript. Premiere on October 27, 1930, Leningrad State Theatre of Opera and Ballet, under baton of A. Gauk.

Op. 23   Two pieces for orchestra (Entr'acte and Finale). 1929. Manuscript.

Op. 24   Music for the comedy "The Shot," by A. Bezymensky. 1929. Manuscript.

Op. 25   Music for the drama "Soil." 1930. Manuscript.

Op. 26   Music for the film "Alone." 1930. Manuscript.

Op. 27   "Bolt"—ballet in three acts. 1930–31. Manuscript. Premiere on April 8, 1931, Leningrad State Theatre of Opera and Ballet, under baton of A. Gauk.

Op. 28   Music for Play "Rule Britannia." 1931. Manuscript.

Op. 29   "Lady Macbeth of Mtsensk"—Opera in Four Acts (Libretto by Y. Preis, based on novel of N. Leskov).

1930–32. Music Publishing House, 1935. Premiere on Jan. 22, 1934, Leningrad Small Opera House, under baton of S. Samosud.

Op. 30 Music for film "Golden Hills" (Suite from music for film, published by Music Publishing House, 1935). 1931. Manuscript.

Op. 31 Music for Sketch "Allegedly Murdered." 1931. Manuscript.

Op. 32 Music for W. Shakespeare's tragedy "Hamlet." 1931–32. Manuscript.

Op. 33 Music for the film "Counterplan" (the theme song was published in the U.S.S.R. by the Music Publishing House and "Triton." In the U.S.A. it was published in 1942 with a new text under the title "United Nations"). 1932. Manuscript.

Op. 34 24 Preludes for Pianoforte. 1932–33. Music Publishing House, 1933.

Op. 35 Concerto for Pianoforte, trumpets and string orchestra. 1933. Music Publishing House, 1934. Premiere on October 15, 1933. Solo by the composer.

Op. 36 Music for the film "Tale of the Priest and His Servant Balda." 1934. Manuscript.

Op. 37 Music for the play "Human Comedy" (based on Balzac). 1933–34. Manuscript.

Op. 38 Suite for Dance Band (Waltz, Polka, Blues). 1934. Manuscript. Premiere on March 24, 1938, Leningrad.

Op. 39 "Bright Rivulet"—Ballet in 3 Acts. 1934. Manuscript. Premiere on June 4, 1935, Leningrad Theatre of Opera and Ballet, under baton of Feldt.

Op. 40 Sonata for Violoncello and Pianoforte. 1934. "Triton" Music Publishing House, 1935.

Op. 41 Music for the film "Girl Friends." 1934. Manuscript.

Op. 42 Five Fragments for Orchestra. 1935. Manuscript.

Op. 43 Fourth Symphony. 1935–36. Manuscript. This symphony was not performed.

Op. 44 Music for Afinogenov's play "Salute to Spain." 1936. Manuscript.

Op. 45 Music for the film "Return of Maxim." 1936–37. Manuscript.

Op. 46 Four Romanzas to the verses of Pushkin ("Resurrection," "To a Youth," "Presentiment," "Stanzas"). 1936. Manuscript.

Op. 47 Fifth Symphony. 1937. Music Publishing House, 1939. Premiere on October 21, 1937, Leningrad Philharmonic, under baton of E. Mravinsky.

Op. 48 Music for the film "Volochayev Days." 1936–37. Manuscript.

Op. 49 Quartet. 1938. Music Publishing House, 1940. Premiere on October 10, 1938, Glazounov Quartet.

Op. 50 Music for the film "Vyborg District." 1938. Manuscript.

Op. 51 Music for the film "Friends." 1938. Manuscript.

Op. 52 Music for the film "The Great Citizen." 1938. Manuscript.

Op. 53 Music for the film "Man with the Gun." 1938. Manuscript.

Op. 54 Sixth Symphony. 1939. Music Publishing House, 1941. Premiere on November 5, 1939, Leningrad Philharmonic, under baton of E. Mravinsky.

Op. 55 Music for the film "The Great Citizen" (second series). 1939. Manuscript.

Op. 56 Music for the film "Silly Little Mouse." 1939. Manuscript.

Op. 57 Quintet (for Pianoforte and Strings). 1940. Published by Union of Soviet Composers, 1941. Premiere on November 23, 1940, Beethoven Quartet and composer.

Op. 58 New orchestration of the opera "Boris Godunov." 1939–40. Manuscript.

Op. 59 Three pieces for violin. 1940. Manuscript.

Op. 60 Seventh Symphony. 1941. Music Publishing House,

1942. Premiere on March 5, 1942, Orchestra of the Bolshoi Theatre, under baton of S. Samosud.

Op. 61   "Leningrad," Suite for choir and orchestra. 1942. Manuscript. Premiere October 15, 1942.

Op. 62   Six romances to the words of Burns, Shakespeare, Walter Raleigh (for Bass and Orchestra). 1942. Published by Union of Soviet Composers, 1943.

Op. 63   "The Players," Opera on theme by Gogol. Manuscript (unfinished).

Op. 64   Piano Sonata No. 2. 1943. Published by State Music Publishing House (MUZGIZ), 1944. Premiere November 11, 1943, author at piano.

Op. 65   Eighth Symphony. 1942. Published by State Music Publishing House (MUZGIZ), 1946. Premiere November 9, 1943, State Symphony Orchestra of the U.S.S.R., under baton of Evgeni Mravinski.

Op. 66   Music for the concert-play "Great River." Manuscript.

Op. 67   Trio for Piano, Violin and Violoncello. 1944. Published by State Music Publishing House (MUZGIZ), 1945. Premiere on November 9, 1944: author at piano, D. Tsiganov—violin, S. Shirinski—violoncello.

Op. 68   Music for the film "Zoya." 1944. Manuscript.

Op. 69   String Quartet No. 2, published by State Music Publishing House (MUZGIZ), 1945. Premiere on November 9, 1944, by the Beethoven Quartet.

Op. 70   Ninth Symphony. 1945. Published by Union of Soviet Composers, 1945. Premiere on November 11, 1945, by Orchestra of Leningrad State Philharmonic, under the baton of Eugene Mravinsky.

Without Opus: Suite for Jazz No. 2. 1938. Manuscript "Oath to the Commissar" (for Choir and Piano). 1942. Published by State Music Publishing House (MUZGIZ), 1942. March for Military Orchestra, 1942. Manuscript.

Six Children's Pieces written for his daughter, Galya.

INDEX

197